The stiff, rice-hull pillow rustled noisily when Eun-Me burrowed her head into a comfortable position.

Filtering under the door, a static-laced broadcast of a traditional folk song crackled from Philip's radio. Eun-Me pictured him on the sofa, his feet propped up on the low coffee table. The image sent another warm shiver through her. He was here. In the next room. She couldn't take her mind off the delightful fact.

For the longest time she had convinced herself that her remembrance of Philip was much more idyllic than the real man. She'd felt certain that, once she saw him face-to-face, the reality of him would shatter the sainted status he held in her mind. In fact, the flesh-and-blood Philip sitting on the sofa far exceeded her idealized memory of him.

Yet even as she contemplated all of Philip's wonderful attributes and relived her joy at seeing him again, a pang of guilt seized her. He belonged to Jennifer.

SUSAN K. DOWNS and her pastor-husband can often be heard speaking Korean in their home. For, although they now reside in Canton, Ohio, the Downs' spent five of their twenty-five years in the ministry as missionaries to Korea, and they adopted two of their five children from Korea. Susan's former career as an international adoption program coordinator expanded her vocabulary to include a few words of Chinese, Vietnamese, and Russian, as well. These days, however, Susan sticks primarily to the use of English for her many fiction and non-fiction writing projects and in her work as a free-lance copy editor.

전수진

(Susan's Korean name)

Remnant of Grace

Susan K. Downs

Heartsong Presents

To my beautiful Korean-born daughters,
Kimberly (Moon-Young) and Courtney (Jeong-Ok).
I thank God for intertwining your lives with mine and,
thereby, expanding our family's cultural heritage to
include *Korea—Land of the Morning Calm.*

A note from the author:
*I love to hear from my readers! You may correspond with me
by writing:* **Susan K. Downs**
Author Relations
PO Box 719
Uhrichsville, OH 44683

ISBN 1-58660-201-2

REMNANT OF GRACE

All Scripture quotations are taken from the King James Version of
the Bible.

All of the characters and events in this book are fictitious. Any
resemblance to actual persons, living or dead, or to actual events
is purely coincidental.

Cover illustration by Victoria Lisi and Julius

PRINTED IN THE U.S.A.

one

Friday, June 23, 1950

Eun-Me scrubbed a year's worth of accumulated dust off the cabin's yellowed linoleum. Her strokes kept cadence with the gentle waves as their natural rhythm lapped a tireless, steady beat against the stretch of Korean shoreline known as Taechon Foreigner's Beach.

While she worked, a constant tide of memories, emotions, and questions flooded her thoughts. Eight years had passed since she stood on the Inchon pier and waved good-bye to Philip as a prisoner of war exchange ship carried him away from Eun-Me's homeland and out to sea.

In those torturous, sweet days before the Japanese expelled all remaining Americans from Korea during World War II, she, her brother, and the missionary's son had been an inseparable trio of best buddies. But, when Philip Woods returned today, would he greet her like a long-lost friend? Or like his parents' household servant—the *ajumoni*—she had since become?

She scolded herself for fretting over such senseless musings. She was foolish to give Dr. Philip a second thought. Yesterday, Clarence and Ruth Woods had gone to the Inchon shipyards, not only to meet Philip, but to also meet their future daughter-in-law, Philip's future bride. Today, after a night's rest at their Seoul home, the Woods family planned to drive down to their cabin at the foreigner's beach along the coast of the South China Sea for a few days of vacation together. For this purpose, Eun-Me had been sent ahead on the train with instructions to air out the cabin and prepare a homecoming celebration feast fit for a king—or a recent medical school graduate who was soon to start his residency.

Eun-Me couldn't imagine a more pleasant assignment. The term "cabin" painted a more rustic word picture than the reality of this beautiful place. She trusted Philip would return with fond memories of the native stone, two-story structure, which included a fully equipped kitchen with American appliances and more modern conveniences than any Korean home.

The clutch of towering firs surrounding the house obscured the waterfront from her view. However, the moment she had removed the winter shutters from the screened porch that ran along the back of the house, fresh ocean breezes lifted the curtains like sails and sent fresh sea air throughout the downstairs rooms. She knew from her previous visits here that the sandy trail leading from the back porch would take her to an isolated swimming beach reserved for missionaries and other expatriates.

Sitting back on her haunches, Eun-Me tossed her scrub brush into the bucket of blackened wash water and looked up to check the time. Two o'clock. The Woods family could arrive from Seoul any minute now, and she had not yet started supper.

She put away her cleaning supplies and scurried about the kitchen, gathering ingredients for the bean paste soup and setting a cast-iron pot full of water on the stove to boil. The spicy meal had been Philip's favorite Korean dish when Eun-Me's mother served as the Woods family's *ajumoni,* and she had helped her mother prepare the aromatic broth for them countless times.

After her mother died of a stroke, Eun-Me had stepped into her position as the Woods family's *ajumoni.* So, now, Eun-Me was the one preparing Philip's favorite dish. And now, instead of being on equal social footing with the missionary's son, she was nothing more than a servant. Or worse, a charity case. An orphan.

Yet, harbored within her deepest desires, Eun-Me dreamed of someday cooking all of Philip Woods's favorite foods, not as an *ajumoni,* but as his wife. In her secret fantasies, she saw herself standing close behind *Moksanim* and *Sahmonim* Woods as they greeted the homecoming Philip. Allowing her imagination free rein, she closed her eyes to picture the young doctor running down the gangplank, scooping her into his arms, begging her to be his bride.

However, Eun-Me knew she would never see her yearnings come true. More than years and miles accounted for the wide gulf that separated them. She couldn't marry anyone—much less Philip Woods. With no relatives left to arrange a marriage and no dowry to offer a husband's family, her prospects for a marital union appeared nil. As an orphan, she would never climb any further than the bottom rung on the ladder of Korean society. She was destined to spend a future of lonely days as an *ajumoni.* And Philip was destined to marry another. An American.

Eun-Me stood and swiped at the front of her baggy *mom-pei* trousers. She both looked and felt like she fit the part of a lowly *ajumoni.* If Philip saw her in these ragged work clothes, he'd most definitely feel sorry for her. She couldn't bear his pity. She decided to change.

Before tending to her personal needs, she surveyed the cabin's interior and smiled. She'd done an admirable job of preparing the place, despite the fact that she'd only arrived on the train the day before.

Eun-Me changed into the only dress she owned besides her traditional Korean *hanbok*—a stylish gold shirtwaist dress that Mrs. Woods had ordered for her last year from a Stateside catalog. Although she probably should have chosen something more conservative, Eun-Me liked the dress's rich color and the stares it solicited when she walked through the South Gate Market on her weekly shopping trips.

She hurriedly tucked and pinned her wayward strands of hair back into place. Then, swiping at the smudges on her face with a palmful of cold water, she shot a cursory glance toward the mirror before heading back to the kitchen to resume her duties at the stove.

The pungent broth of garlic, hot peppers, and bean paste had just come to a rolling boil when the crunch of automobile tires on the gravel road jarred Eun-Me into a kinetic frenzy. Philip had arrived. And he was calling for her.

Philip struggled through the cabin's screen door with Jennifer's oversized suitcase. "*Yoboseyo?* Hello? Grace? You here?"

Without waiting for a response, he dropped his burden in the entryway, shucked off his loafers, stepped over the neat row of house slippers, and padded quietly down the hallway in his stocking feet toward the kitchen. The sinus-clearing smells of long-forgotten Oriental delicacies greeted him and, in that mouthwatering moment, he knew he had come home to Korea.

He recognized her soft voice before she appeared in the kitchen doorway, and he couldn't help but smile at her unique blending of Korean and English—"Konglish," they had called it as kids.

"*Anyong haseyo, Paksanim* Philip! Welcome home." She shuffled toward him, her form already bent in a deep bow.

"Hey, Grace. Don't waste those honorific titles on me." He engulfed her dainty shoulder in his palm, hoping to still her incessant dipping and nodding. "I'm not 'Doctor' to you. It's just me, your ol' buddy Phil. Now, stop your kow-towing and come give me a good American-style hello hug."

Philip bit back a smile as he stooped over to gather her into his arms. He almost told her that she was just as short as he remembered her, but decided this was not the time. He pulled her close and buried his face in her hair. Her sweet essence stirred within him pleasant remembrances of his dear childhood friend, and he drew a deep breath, savoring the memories. Yet, even in the midst of the nostalgic pleasure he found in Grace's embrace, guilt stabbed at his conscience to find such joy in the arms of any woman other than his fiancée.

He could feel tension emanating from Grace, making him wonder if she felt his sudden attack of conviction, or if her stiff reaction was simply a result of his breach of Korean etiquette. He hoped their reunion held the same significance for her as it did for him. The last thing he wanted was for Grace to feel that their friendship must end since he would soon be a married man.

He released her and she immediately backed away two

short steps. He heard Jennifer and his parents clamoring through the front door, and he knew he should hurry to help them with the luggage, but he lingered to study Grace's face.

Over the course of his lengthy absence, she had passed from adolescence to adulthood. Her unblemished complexion and rosebud lips still needed no assistance from cosmetic jars or lipstick tubes to enhance her beauty. Yet, her almond eyes, which once sparked with mischievous fire, now radiated a silent sorrow.

Philip couldn't help but question why God had permitted wave after wave of tragedy and suffering to sweep over one as gentle and meek as Grace. At the age of ten, she'd been forced to witness her pastor-father's execution by the Japanese occupying forces when he refused to bow to the Shinto shrine. Surely that was enough trauma to last a lifetime, yet there was more.

Shortly after his parents reentered Korea following Japan's surrender to the Allied forces, they wrote Philip with news about Grace's brother, Eun-Soo. Evidently, about the same time the Woods family was forced to leave Korea during World War II, the Japanese had conscripted Eun-Soo to work in a Manchurian coal mine. Soon after, Grace and her mother received a one-line telegram announcing that Eun-Soo had died in a mining accident. No further explanation ever came concerning his mysterious demise.

The impact of his good friend's death had not fully hit him until this moment. Never again would he laugh at Eun-Soo's antics. Their "Trio of Trouble" was no more.

Now, Grace had been forced to bear the grief of her mother's death as well. Even though he had sent her letters expressing his sympathies, he wanted to further convey his continued sorrow.

"About Eun-Soo—and your *omma*—" Philip's throat clogged with emotion and his words tapered off to a whisper.

"No, no, *Paksanim* Phil." Grace shook her head back and forth and raised her palms toward him. "Don't say anymore. Save your sadness for another time. This is a happy day, and you mustn't spoil it by dwelling on things we can't change." She then hid her brilliant smile behind her hand, in typical Korean fashion, yet she seemed to deliberately avoid eye contact with him.

"I'll unpack your things and you can rest." Her words came at a fast clip. "I have your old room all ready for you." She moved to slip by him, but he stopped her before she could escape his reach.

"Wait. I can unpack my own things. Besides, there is someone I really want you to meet." His fingers softly encircled her forearm, and he led her down the hall to the entryway.

❦

Eun-Me forced a smile. She wasn't sure she was ready to be introduced to the woman he had pledged to marry.

She nodded and bowed in greeting to *Moksanim* and *Sahmonim* Woods, who stood in the stairwell leading off the entryway. They sloughed effortlessly out of their street shoes and clamored up the stairs, each lugging a suitcase behind them.

A slender figure sat in the middle of the shoe-cluttered entryway, struggling to untie the laces of her shoes. Hoping to catch a quick glimpse of the woman, Eun-Me craned her neck from side to side, then up and down. The stranger's chin-length, curly blond hair fell into her face, preventing Eun-Me from getting a clear view, yet that which she could see looked stunning.

From beneath the hair, Eun-Me heard a shaky voice. "I don't know how my shoelaces got so tangled. And I don't think I should have to trade my own sneakers for some used straw slippers, anyway. Who knows who wore them before me? Just think of the germs! As I recall, you said this place would be just like an American home. I never have to take off my shoes at home in San Francisco."

The woman abandoned her attempts to untie her shoes and yanked them off, tossing them toward the door. She donned a pair of woven bamboo slippers, then stared at her feet in a lengthy silence.

Abruptly, the American lady tipped her head back and sniffed at the air with a crinkled nose. "Has there been a skunk nearby?"

Eun-Me leaned to whisper to Philip. "I don't know. What is a skunk?"

At her words, Philip's lips tightened and his cheeks darkened.

Eun-Me squirmed, hoping against her common sense that the question bore no correlation to the smell of the bean paste soup simmering on the stove. In her eagerness to provide a warm welcome for Philip, she hadn't stopped to consider how someone unaccustomed to Korean food might react to this particularly puissant odor while it cooked.

She longed to slink off and hide. If she made a hasty retreat, she could postpone these introductions until Philip's pretty fiancée had recovered from her exhausting journey and was in a better mood.

Eun-Me frantically glanced around the room, planning her getaway. However, before she could slip out of the room, Philip cleared his throat in readiness to speak. Eun-Me waved her hands in a frantic attempt to stop him, but he replied despite her protests.

"The skunk is a unique animal that is native to North America. I'll explain later." He turned to Jennifer and gave her a smile that Eun-Me knew was forced. "Hey, Jennifer. Forget about the shoes and the smells for now. There's someone here I'd like you to meet."

The woman rose from the floor to tower over Eun-Me. With one hand, she flipped her blond hair out of her face, then raked her fingers through her curls to smooth them into place.

Eun-Me waited for Philip to begin the honors of a formal introduction, but before he could speak, his fiancée stepped forward. In response, Eun-Me automatically dipped in a low honorific bow, but as she straightened, Jennifer's descending hand smacked her in the nose, bringing stars to her eyes.

She stood quickly, blinking away the sting and forcing herself to keep her hands at her side instead of checking for blood, which would further bring attention to the woman's awkwardness.

Jennifer rubbed her own hand as she spoke. "Oops. Sorry. I'm a bit off-kilter and not used to all this bowing," she said, her voice increasing in volume, and slowing in tempo with each word.

"Can you speak English?" Jennifer shouted. Jennifer pressed her index finger into the center of her chest. "Jennifer." She pointed to Eun-Me. "What's your name?" Her voice slowed even more, but the volume of her voice leveled. "Do. You. Understand. Me?"

Eun-Me stretched to her full height, but she was still much shorter than the tall, slender Jennifer. Before she could speak, Philip rested his hand on Jennifer's shoulder.

"Jennifer, you don't need to shout," he said in a flat, even tone that Eun-Me had only heard him use when he was very, very angry. "I'm the only one in the room with a hearing loss and I can hear you loud and clear." While he spoke, he fingered the thin scar that split his cheek in front of his ear, and his subtle motion served as a forceful reminder to Eun-Me of his old prisoner-of-war injury.

"Grace isn't deaf, and she speaks English better than many of the kids in our own schools in the States. Jennifer Anderson, this is Cho, Eun-Me."

Eun-Me forced herself not to bow again, and at the same time, did her best to control her voice so that it held no hint of an Asian accent, especially after Philip's high praise of her language skills. "I am very pleased to make your acquaintance, Miss Anderson."

Jennifer stiffened, her mouth tightened, and her eyebrows raised. First she glanced at Philip, then back to Eun-Me. "I'm pleased to meet you, Miss Me. You are the first real Korean I've met, except for the crew on the freighter coming over. You don't mind if I call you Cho Eun, do you?"

Not sure how to respond, Eun-Me stared at the floor until Philip broke the silence.

"Her name isn't Miss Me. If you want to use her Korean name, you should address her either as 'Miss Cho' or 'Eun-Me.' Koreans place the family name first and the given name last, and each given name has a special meaning.

Eun-Me's name means Grace and Beauty. So, when she asked my dad to give her an English biblical name, as many Korean Christians do, 'Grace' seemed to be the perfect fit for Eun-Me.

"Rather than using her Korean name, you might find it easier to call her Grace. And, in return, she should call you Jennifer. You wouldn't mind that, would you, Grace?"

Grace raised her attention from the floor, back to Jennifer. "No. Not at all. Philip has always called me 'Grace,' and I'd be honored if you'd do the same." Eun-Me tried to smile in encouragement toward Jennifer. However, the gesture of friendship was not reciprocated. Instead, Jennifer turned to glare at Philip, and as she spoke, tears slid down her cheeks.

"How could you embarrass me like that, Philip?" She shook visibly as she spoke. "I thought the servants weren't to call us by our first names. And now, this last-name-first thing! I can't be expected to know all these funny little rules."

At the word "servant," Philip immediately stiffened from head to toe. Before he could speak, Eun-Me stepped forward and laid her hand lightly on Jennifer's arm. Jennifer flinched at her touch, so Eun-Me backed up a step, completing the break in contact. "There is no need to feel embarrassed. The Korean culture and language are very different from yours, and you are in a strange land. No one expects you to know these things immediately. I've been studying English since I was ten, but I still make many humiliating blunders."

"Your English is impeccable, Grace," Philip interrupted. "And I'm not ashamed to take a good part of the credit for teaching you." He turned to face his fiancée, his posture remaining rigid as he spoke. "You've heard my stories about Grace and her family since the day we met. She's not just a housekeeper or *servant*," he said, enunciating the word very clearly. "She's an old family friend."

Distress clouded Jennifer's eyes. Eun-Me wished there was something she could do to set the pretty lady at ease but couldn't think of anything other than to show the honored guest to her room.

"You must be exhausted after such a long boat trip from America. I can turn down your bed so you can rest."

Philip suddenly relaxed his posture and stepped up to Jennifer, laying an arm around her shoulders.

"I'm sorry. I didn't mean to embarrass you. I suppose it's my fault for not explaining some of these cultural differences better. I keep forgetting how new all this is for you. And you may not have realized that Grace was the childhood friend I'm often talking about. Come on. Give me a little hug and show me that you accept my apology."

When Jennifer turned into Philip to receive his hug, it was Eun-Me's turn to feel embarrassed.

She looked away and squirmed uncomfortably as she witnessed Philip's tenderness toward Jennifer. Their embrace reminded Eun-Me of the welcome hug that Philip had given her just moments earlier. His touch had ricocheted through her like a jolt of electricity that left her trembling from head to toe.

She couldn't remember the last time she'd been held by another human being. Certainly not since her *omma* had died. . .

Oh, how wonderful it would be to rest in the arms of

another. In Philip's arms.

She had loved him since they were children and had suffered an obsessive teenage crush over him even after he left the country when she was fifteen. Since then, no man had ever shown her the respect and admiration that Philip had.

No man paid her any attention at all. In his absence, she had allowed her love for him to grow untethered in the secret places of her heart. She craved his touch, any show of affection, no matter how small.

But, he belonged to another now. She could never enjoy his caress. Besides, only in fairy tales could a housemaid win the heart of a doctor.

Eun-Me shook her head to clear away the nonsensical thought. She didn't have time for such absurd daydreams. She had work to do. Easing away from the private exchange between Philip and Miss Anderson, Eun-Me excused herself with a muttered explanation that she never expected them to hear.

"If you'll pardon me, I'll just run along and turn back that bed for Miss Jennifer now."

❦

From over the top of Jennifer's shoulder, Philip watched Grace disappear down the hallway.

The sound of his father's deep baritone voice above him made him jump.

"Hey, you two, knock it off. You aren't alone, you know."

Philip released Jennifer and looked up to see his parents descending the stairs. "Sorry, Dad. But I had some apologizing to do. I seem to recall you having to beg forgiveness from Mom a time or two."

"No comment." Philip's dad ducked his head to avoid a

playful slap from his mother as she came up behind him.

"Watch it, Mr. Missionary, or I'll go sunbathing without you. I saw our bachelor missionary, Richard Spencer, laying on the beach when we pulled into the compound. I bet he knows how to treat a missionary mama right."

"I'm not about to let a gorgeous dame like you out of my sight."

Philip watched as his dad flicked a beach towel at his mom. Two years had passed since his parents returned to Korea, leaving him in San Francisco to finish medical school. His heart warmed to watch them banter playfully with one another again. He breathed a silent prayer that his marriage would be as strong as his parents' union after thirty years together.

He turned to Jennifer, a wide grin spreading over his face. "Looks like the old folks are heading for a swim. You feel up to a dip in the drink?"

"Sure," she responded. But the smile she returned seemed to tax her energies to their limits.

"Hey, if you're too tired, I understand. If you want, I'll set up the beach umbrella, and you can take a nap in the fresh ocean air. I could lie beside you and work on my tan awhile. With the hours I've been keeping at the hospital lately, I've not seen the sun for months."

"Truth is, Philip, after two weeks on an ocean liner, I've breathed about all the sea air I can stand, and my stomach is doing flip-flops. Why don't you go to the beach with your parents? I'll catch up with you after I've had a chance to rest a bit."

Philip's mother wagged a finger in his face. "Son, you may have all the fancy letters after your name and an expensive doctor education, but you need to listen to a little advice from ol' Mom and let this girl sleep as long as she wants in a real, on-solid-ground bed. She was too keyed up to get a good rest last night in Seoul, and she looks plumb worn out."

She stroked Jennifer's hair with a mother's tender touch as she continued her lecture and, although she'd not been back to her native Texas for more than thirty years, a strong south-Texan twang still peppered her speech. "We've got all summer to visit, and you can stand to be away from her for an hour or so. Why don't you carry her suitcase into her bedroom and help her get settled, then join us at the shore by the boat launch in just a bit? Eun-Me will take good care of Jennifer while we're gone. Goodness gracious, we won't be far."

He was about to ask Jennifer if that was what she would prefer, but when he looked at her, the dark circles under her eyes and her drooping shoulders told him all he needed to know.

"All right, Jennifer. As your personal physician, and after consultation with my esteemed colleague, I am ordering complete bed rest for you." Her suitcase stood just inside the entryway where he'd abandoned it earlier, and he moved to pick it up. His words trailed after him while he dragged the weighty luggage down the hallway. "I'll have to answer to your dad when we return Stateside, so I've got to take good care of you. When we get back to San Francisco in August, it wouldn't do to present a sickly daughter to the doctor in charge of my residency."

Jennifer shuffled her feet as she walked behind him but paused at the bathroom door halfway down the hall. "Don't be ridiculous, Philip. You can do no wrong in Daddy's eyes. Now, if you'll excuse me for just a moment—"

She closed the bathroom door behind her while Philip craned his good ear toward the other room to catch his mother's words. "We'll run along and see you in a few minutes, Son." The screen door screeched closed behind them, and he could hear their flip-flops slapping against the sandy path as they headed down to the shore.

When he entered the guest bedroom, he found Grace in front of an open window, waving a towel. "What on earth are you doing, Gracie?"

"I fear that these cooking odors have made your fiancée sick, so I'm trying to shake out some of the smell. I should have stayed with my plan to serve the *bulgogi*. But I remembered how you liked the bean paste soup—I didn't even stop to think how your fiancée might react to our more potent Korean foods."

"Grace, the sooner Jennifer acclimates herself to Korea, the better. And the soup smells wonderful to me. I can't wait till supper. I've not had a decent Korean meal since I left Seoul eight years ago. And Dad says your *kimchee* is even better than your *omma*'s." Philip watched as the second-hand compliment sent a shy smile tugging at the corners of Grace's lips.

"In fact," he continued, "I wish you'd teach Jennifer your secret to making good *kimchee*. That's one of the reasons I brought her to Korea—so she'd learn how to cook Korean food. A basic prerequisite for any woman who hopes to marry me is the ability to produce a tasty pot of *kimchee* now and then."

An undercurrent of a chuckle tinted her reply. "I am

happy to help you in any way that I can. You know that. But we'd better postpone the cooking lessons awhile. Miss Jennifer doesn't look like she could stomach much more of our culture today."

At that moment, Jennifer walked into the room and sat on the corner of the bed, her shoulders sagging. "You've got that right, Honey. My tummy's upset. And my head is killing me. If you'd fetch me a glass of water and a spoon, I could stir up a bicarbonate of soda. Then, I really need to sleep."

Philip tightened his lips, not liking the way Jennifer again summarily dismissed his old friend. As he watched Grace obediently bow out of the room to retrieve the requested items, he determined to discuss the matter with Jennifer after her nap.

"Rest well, Jennifer." He paused at the doorway as he spoke. "Since things seem to be under control here, I'm going to change into my swim trunks and spend a bit of time with my folks on the beach."

In less than three minutes, he had rifled through his luggage for his swimsuit, changed, and grabbed a clean beach towel from the bathroom on his way out the door. As he rounded the corner of the cabin and stepped onto the sandy trail leading to the beach, a volley of rifle fire rang through the air. And a woman's scream sliced through the cabin walls.

two

Jennifer's shrieks brought Eun-Me racing back to the bed-room from the kitchen.

"Oh, God, have mercy on me! We're under attack! I don't want to die! Where's Philip? Why did he insist on bringing me here?"

Eun-Me rounded the corner to see the distraught American on her knees in the middle of the bed, clutching the bodice of her housecoat. Eun-Me froze in her tracks as she tried to decide how to handle the situation.

Philip couldn't have gotten far down the trail to the beach. However, if she ran to catch him, she'd have to leave Jennifer alone. That didn't seem like a wise idea in light of Jennifer's distraught condition.

Eun-Me hesitantly approached the bed, one arm out-stretched. "Everything is all right, Miss Jennifer."

As Eun-Me continued to approach her, Jennifer recoiled. Not knowing what else to do until Philip arrived, Eun-Me decided to speak from across the room. She lowered her voice in an attempt to calm Miss Jennifer without touching her. "We're not under attack. Listen to me. No one is shooting at us."

"What was that, then?" Jennifer narrowed her eyes to a harsh squint, making Eun-Me feel that Jennifer somehow held her personally responsible for the commotion.

"The gunfire comes from the military outpost on the back

side of the beach. The troops practice maneuvers there every afternoon. You'll get used to the ruckus soon enough. Please. Trust me. We're all right. Everything is all right."

Jennifer's chin quivered when she spoke. "I want Philip. Find him for me. And hurry."

As though cued, Philip burst into the room. Jennifer's tears erupted again when he gathered her in his arms.

Eun-Me offered a hurried repeat explanation of the explosion to Philip, but before she could go into more detail about the military exercises, Jennifer interrupted her as she pushed away from Philip. "I can't take this. Why did I ever let you convince me to come? I'm already a nervous wreck. I'll never survive a whole summer."

"Listen, Jennifer. This is the first I've heard of any military exercises, but rather than fussing about the noise, let's thank God for the protection and safety these troops give us."

Eun-Me watched Jennifer send Philip an incredulous glare, then sputter, "But. . .but. . ."

He held up a hand to silence her. "You've gotten yourself all worked up. Let me get my bag and dig out a mild sedative to help you sleep." Philip darted out of the room, leaving Eun-Me to watch over Jennifer. He returned within seconds, however, clutching two white capsules in the palm of his hand.

A staccato rat-a-tat of rifle fire sounded in the distance as he persuaded Jennifer to lie back down. Minutes after downing the pills, her breathing became rhythmic and steady as she dozed off.

Philip waited a few more minutes to make certain Jennifer was sleeping soundly before he excused himself to join his parents at the beach.

"I don't expect Jennifer to wake up for hours," he said to Eun-Me as she walked with him to the back door. "But if she does, just ring the dinner bell and I'll come running."

❦

Long after Eun-Me had cleared the table and put away the leftovers, Philip and his parents remained in their seats. Eun-Me snatched glimpses of the laughing, reminiscing family as she washed the dishes and tidied the kitchen. There could be no denying that Philip was his parents' son. He had inherited his mother's sandy blond hair and pewter gray eyes, his father's imposing six-foot, three-inch height and dimpled chin.

When a loud belch escaped from *Moksanim* Woods, Philip tipped back his head and roared with laughter. "You sure know how to compliment the cook, Dad. And you have proven once again that you are more Korean than American."

Moksanim's chair screeched against the linoleum floor as he pushed back and rose to loom over Eun-Me. "I can't find words to say it any more eloquently, Grace. You really outdid yourself on that fantastic dinner." Philip stood and sandwiched Eun-Me between the two of them.

"Add my amen to that, Grace. I wish I could have polished off the last of that *kimchee,* but I'm too stuffed. Don't be surprised if you hear me raiding the refrigerator in the middle of the night, though." He picked up his coffee cup and motioned to his folks with a jerk of his head. "What do you say we take our coffee to the davenport and relax awhile? I'd like to see if I can pick up any stations on my transistor radio. I need to brush up a little on my

Korean listening skills."

As Eun-Me poured fresh coffee into their cups, her muscles ached with such fatigue that she had to steady the pot with both hands. After fighting back several yawns, she finally found the courage to ask *Sahmonim* Woods if she could retire early for the evening.

"Should Miss Jennifer wake up, I've left a light supper for her in the icebox."

"You run along to bed, Dear," *Sahmonim* urged. "We can take care of Jennifer."

Philip stood in polite deference to Eun-Me as she bowed and backed out of the living room. "Judging from the looks of Jennifer when I checked earlier, she may sleep the rest of the night, but thank you for all you've done to make her feel comfortable. And, Grace—it's wonderful to see you again."

A shiver of excitement raced through her as she looked into his eyes. She swallowed hard. Licked her lips. And whispered a breathy, "You, too."

Dropping her gaze, she fled to her makeshift sleeping quarters in the storage room off the kitchen. She latched the door behind her and buried her head in her hands. If her *omma* were here, she would have undoubtedly launched into Eun-Me with a rapid-fire Korean tongue-lashing by now.

"Remember your station, Daughter," she would have said. "Master the art of self-control. Never allow your emotions free rein." And *Omma* would have been right on all counts.

Yet her heart refused to listen to logic and reason in matters concerning Philip Woods.

She unrolled her pallet and smoothed the bedding before

climbing under the covers of the thick *yoh*. The stiff, rice-hull pillow rustled noisily when Eun-Me burrowed her head into a comfortable position. Filtering under the door, a static-laced broadcast of a traditional folk song crackled from Philip's radio. Eun-Me pictured him on the sofa, his feet propped up on the low coffee table. The image sent another warm shiver through her. He was here. In the next room. She couldn't take her mind off the delightful fact.

For the longest time, she had convinced herself that her remembrance of Philip was much more idyllic than the real man. She felt certain that, once she saw him face-to-face, the reality of him would shatter the sainted status he held in her mind. In fact, the flesh-and-blood Philip sitting on the sofa far exceeded her revered memory of him.

Yet, even as she contemplated all of Philip's wonderful attributes and relived her joy at seeing him again, a pang of guilt seized her. He belonged to Jennifer.

She needed help in sorting out her feelings, and there was only one place she knew to turn for wisdom and guidance. Eun-Me reached into the kerchief-bound bundle of her belongings, which sat on the floor by her mat, and withdrew her Korean/English Bible. The pages fell open to the bookmarked place in the Book of James.

Breathing a prayer for inspiration, she picked up her reading where she'd left off yesterday. As she'd gotten into the habit of doing, she focused first on the English version of the passage and tried to see if she could catch the meaning of the verse without reading the Korean translation. Despite her weariness, the wealth of insight contained in the few phrases she read grabbed her attention, and she tried hard to concentrate, but she read no further than the first chapter, when her eyelids drooped shut. She weakly tried to open them again, but the effort proved too great.

❦

Eun-Me blinked back to wakefulness and stared wide-eyed into the blackness for several long seconds as she struggled to place her whereabouts. Not until she heard whispered English coming through the wide crack beneath the storage room door did she remember that she was at the beach cabin. She recognized the voices of Philip and Miss Jennifer and the light, which jabbed at the darkness from under the door, seemed to carry their speech. For, despite their lowered pitch, she understood their every word.

"What are you doing up in the middle of the night, Philip? I'm too keyed up to sleep and my growling stomach doesn't help, either. I'm starving." With a vacuum-sealed thump, the refrigerator slammed shut. "Isn't there anything in this kitchen that I can eat besides that skunk-smelly soup, fermented cabbage, or globby, sticky rice? Where's the peanut butter?"

Eun-Me bit her lip to stifle a rising bubble of indignation. Despite her professed hunger, Miss Jennifer couldn't even bring herself to taste a single bite of the Korean food, yet she was quick to criticize. Either Miss Jennifer fancied herself an extremely finicky eater or she was rather stubborn and set in her ways. Regardless, pleasing her presented Eun-Me with a formidable and unwelcome challenge.

The repeated creak and slam of cabinet doors told Eun-Me that Miss Jennifer's search for food had not yet proven successful.

"Knock it off, Jennifer."

Philip's clipped command caught Eun-Me off guard.

"What?" Jennifer stretched the word into a whine. "What'd I do?"

"You've expressed loud and clear your unhappiness about coming here. That's what."

She pictured Philip in her mind's eye as he drew a long, deep breath, hesitant and uneasy in the task of admonishing his fiancée.

"Jennifer, what's gotten into you? I've never known you to behave like this. Where is that perky, sweet girl who stole my heart? Can't you make the slightest effort?" The intensity of his obvious vexation rose with each question until all indications of his awkwardness were quickly smothered by blatant ire.

"I don't know what you were expecting, but I tried to prepare you. You just didn't want to bother to listen. Don't you realize how condescending you seem? I've held my tongue until now, because I know how stressful this trip has been on you. But you have to realize that when you belittle the food and customs of Korea, you insult me. And another thing—"

Evidently, Philip had realized his growing pitch, for his words suddenly dropped back to a hoarse whisper, and Eun-Me had to strain to catch the next sentence.

"Whether you meant to or not, you've degraded an old family friend by putting on pompous airs. I highly doubt that in the entire course of your lifetime you will ever have to experience the hardships that Grace has already endured."

Once again, Philip abandoned his efforts to keep his voice down as his volume rose with his emotions. "I owe a lot to Grace and I won't have you demeaning her. She's one of the most selfless people you'll ever meet. In fact, she's even sleeping on the storage room floor right now so that you could have some privacy."

When she heard him say her name, Grace's ears heated with embarrassment. His words weren't meant for her to hear and she felt like a spy, eavesdropping like this. Still, she couldn't very well interrupt their discussion now. She rolled to her side and covered her head with one arm in an unsuccessful attempt to block out Philip's diatribe. No one had asked her to sleep in the storage room. She had made the choice in order to afford Miss Jennifer some comfort and privacy as she adjusted to her new surroundings. And she did not regret her decision, nor did she expect Miss Jennifer's gratitude. Yet, she knew that if she had done the same for Philip, he would have gone out of his way to express his thanks.

"Let me remind you that, up until the prisoner-of-war exchange, Grace was the one who brought us word from home along with our meals every day during the six months that Dad and I were imprisoned. She nursed my wounds and bandaged my ear after each interrogation and beating. During that time, she and her mother stayed, at the risk of great peril, to look after my mom while she was under house arrest. And, long before her mother came to work for us, her father was my dad's best friend."

At the mention of her father, tears stung Eun-Me's eyes and she whisked them away with a quick swipe of her elbow while Philip's voice took on a tender tone.

"When Pastor Cho and his wife became Christians, their parents disowned them for refusing to worship Buddha or practice Shamanism and ancestor worship. So, our family took the place of the Chos' own flesh and blood. After Pastor Cho died a martyr's death, we brought Grace, Eun-Soo, and their *omma* into our home, since their kin had rejected them. Grace is no servant to us. She's family. Do you understand?"

Gooseflesh erupted on Eun-Me's arms when she heard Philip refer to her as "family." Perhaps she wasn't as alone as she had assumed herself to be after *Omma*'s death. She heard a distinct tinge of brotherly affection in Philip's words as he continued.

"So, if you can't find it within yourself to befriend her, at least grant her the respect she deserves. Neither she nor her mother has ever been treated like a servant, and I won't stand for your condescending airs now. I love you, Jennifer. But I have to tell you, I felt pretty disappointed in you today."

In the long silence that followed, Eun-Me tried to picture Jennifer's reaction to Philip's scolding. She raised up onto one elbow and listened for sniffles that would indicate an encore of this afternoon's tears. Was she crying? Pouting? Or cowering? Expecting to hear a soft, apologetic response, Eun-Me winced at Miss Jennifer's sharp rebuttal.

"Look. I'm sorry. Okay? I know I've been cranky and critical. But you have to remember, I've never been outside of California. Give me some time to get used to all this. Nothing makes sense to me. On one hand, I'm scared to death, and on the other—well, frankly, I find it all so pathetic. Oxen and field workers in funny hats and thatched roofed huts and primitive conditions, just like a page out of a *National Geographic,* but with machine-gun-toting military guys thrown in. You grew up around here. You're used to all this noise and smell and war-game business."

"You're wrong there, Miss Jennifer," Eun-Me muttered to herself, for she knew from a lifetime of personal experience that no one ever gets used to war. She had spent her whole life under the heavy-handed rule of the Japanese, and she felt certain that, until her dying day, she would cringe at the sight of a pea green uniform. Surely, Philip must feel even more fearful than she for, following Japan's bombing of Pearl Harbor and their official declaration of war against America, Philip had been arrested and interned on trumped-up spy charges. He had suffered through six months of physical beatings and emotional tortures before his repatriation back to the States.

"We probably ought to postpone this discussion until tomorrow." Philip's voice held a note of weary resignation. "I'm afraid that we've already disturbed Grace's sleep, and you need to eat something before you make yourself sick. Although you aren't likely to find anything to your liking in the cupboards. They don't sell peanut butter anywhere around here. However, you should be happy to know that I had the foresight to pack a couple of jars of peanut butter. I'll run upstairs and grab a jar from my suitcase so you can make us both a sandwich."

As his footsteps carried him away from the kitchen, the volume of his words dropped. "While I'm gone, why don't you go and rest on the davenport? Flip on my radio if you want. That's what I do when I'm keyed up and having trouble sleeping. But, Jennifer, please. . .try to learn why it is that I love this land and these people so."

"Okay, Philip. I'll try harder. But I'm still so nervous

and shaky. Could I get you to give me another dose of that mild sedative you gave me this afternoon? Maybe everything will look better after a few more hours of sleep."

❦

Saturday, June 24, 1950

The clapper on Eun-Me's windup alarm clock jangled obnoxiously to signal her 4:45 wake-up time. Despite the short night, she wanted to slip over to the open-air tabernacle for her daily dawn prayer time before she began her workday.

She changed from her nightgown into her *mom-pei* trousers and a shapeless work shirt, then crept softly through the house with her shoes in hand so as not to disturb the others. The skies, although dry at the moment, couldn't be trusted to stay that way in the middle of rainy season, and the trees still dripped with the vestiges of a midnight shower. She sprouted her umbrella, then tucked her Bible into the crook of her free arm and set out down the sandy path.

Eun-Me veered to the left when she came to a fork in the trail, and her steps fell silent as she traveled over a blanket of pine needles, picking her way through the underbrush that had yet to be cleared for the summer. The chapel, situated on a bluff, overlooked a rocky portion of shoreline and afforded a breathtaking view of the sea as slender shards of predawn light splintered the dark waves.

Entering the back of the simple sanctuary, Eun-Me discovered that, unfortunately, she was not alone. As her eyes adjusted to the dark room, she recognized the unmistakable silhouette of Philip kneeling at the mourner's bench in front of the pulpit. From what she could see of him, he didn't look like he had slept at all during the night.

Hoping not to disturb Philip's time of prayer, she quietly slid into a seat on the wooden bench nearest the rear door. She debated whether or not she should leave the building altogether and grant Philip total privacy, but before she could decide what to do, the door spring squeaked softly, and *Moksanim* Woods stepped inside. She nodded in greeting as he passed her on his way down the aisle. Then, folding her hands in her lap, she bowed her head and hunched her shoulders, assuming her customary praying posture.

Try as she might, however, she could not channel her thoughts heavenward, for Philip's supplications filled the morning air, and all of Eun-Me's attentions focused on him.

"Dear God, please show me what to do." His rich voice echoed across the chapel. "Oh, Father, I've made such a mess of things. None of this has turned out like I'd hoped. How can I possibly tell her now?"

She jerked forward in an effort to rise. Concern for her troubled friend compelled her to stay. Yet, she didn't want to embarrass him, and Eun-Me felt certain Philip was unaware that others were privy to his prayers. She looked up in time to see Philip's father move in beside him and slip an arm around his shoulder.

"*Hahnahnim, kamsahaomnieda*—Oh, Lord, thank You." She breathed a prayer of gratitude that *Moksanim* had the sensitivity to make his presence known. No doubt, he would counsel Philip concerning whatever mess he felt he had created. She couldn't fathom what it could be. Nor did she feel comfortable knowing unless he shared the matter directly with her. As the two men huddled in holy conversation,

Eun-Me noiselessly tiptoed outside.

Not yet ready to return to the cabin, she stood over-looking the steep staircase that led from the chapel to the beach.

Philip's prayer played repeatedly in her mind. Who was this "her" he had mentioned? What information did he feel hopelessly unable to disclose?

Breathing deeply, she captured a gust of salty wind in her lungs. This guessing game was a waste of her time. If the matter concerned her at all, she'd learn the answers in due time. Until then, she'd redouble her prayers for Philip.

For the moment, she needed to concern herself with the more pressing urgency of breakfast preparations. Fish head soup with steaming sticky rice comprised a typical morning's menu. Usually, a guest would be granted the honor of receiving the fish's eyes in their bowl. However, Eun-Me didn't think that Miss Jennifer would appreciate the time-honored tradition. For today, she decided that she would serve a breakfast of biscuits and gravy and scrambled eggs as something that would better suit Miss Jenni-fer's taste.

Eun-Me traipsed down the steep stairs and onto the beach, headed toward the row of market stalls on the distant horizon. Despite the early hour, she hoped that the egg lady might be open for business.

❧

Throughout breakfast, Philip listened to Jennifer as she gushed on and on with effusive praise of Grace's cooking. He doubted that he was the only one to question the sincerity of her feast-or-famine kindness. Still, he realized she was making a concerted effort to rectify her behavior of yesterday, and for that he was thankful.

His overly animated fiancée had sashayed out of her bedroom and plopped a hefty stack of ladies' magazines and bridal catalogues on the kitchen table. With one look at the pile, he knew why he'd been forced to drag her suitcase all the way down the gangplank.

When Jennifer asked his mother her opinion of pink organza for the bridesmaids' gowns, Philip took her question as his cue to leave. His dad was tinkering with the temperamental hot-water heater in the bathroom and couldn't break away. Grace had left the cabin on an undisclosed errand minutes before. So, collecting his beach towel, folding chair, a half-finished paperback book, and a jug of iced tea, he headed for the shore alone.

He looked forward to burrowing into the warm sand for a snooze under the midmorning sun. The Lord knew he had not gotten much rest of late, but he couldn't blame his sleeplessness on the grueling schedule he'd kept as an emergency room intern. The root of his insomnia stemmed from a growing and dreadful fear that he may have made a horrific misjudgment in his choice of a life mate.

Within the safe haven of her hometown, the daughter of a prestigious San Francisco doctor had seemed like the ideal match for him. He'd found so many reasons to fall in love with Jennifer. Witty and pretty and at ease among the city's most elite social circles, she drew admiring glances wherever they went, and Philip was always proud to be seen with her. Of even more importance to him, she professed a relationship with Jesus Christ and claimed Him as her Savior.

Since that evening last September, when Dr. Anderson had introduced them to one another at a hospital fund-raiser,

Jennifer had always acted enthralled when Philip related one of his childhood adventures as a missionary kid. He thought she found his Korean heritage fascinating and unique. But they had no sooner pulled away from San Francisco Harbor than she set about subtly belittling and berating his adopted motherland. When he described a centuries-old custom, her blank stare plainly conveyed her disinterest. If he tried to teach her a Korean greeting, she floundered like a fish on dry land.

He attributed her anomalous responses to an attempt to mask her ignorance concerning this culture so foreign from her own. Or perhaps she felt a genuine fear of the unknown. Regardless of the cause for her insensitivity, over the course of the two-week voyage, his patience had been stretched tissue-paper thin. And after coming ashore yesterday, their relationship appeared to be deteriorating at an alarming speed. Jennifer's calloused treatment of Grace had dealt a crushing blow. Yet, he couldn't fully explain to her why.

Long before he had invited her to Korea to meet his parents, he had wanted to share with her the other reason he wanted to make this trip. The most important reason. Yet, the right moment for such a disclosure just never seemed to come.

Philip laid his armload of beach paraphernalia on the sun-warmed sand and spread out his towel. Then, stretching his arms toward the sky, he dipped left and right, backward and forward, popping the kinks out of his neck and back. Yesterday when he'd come here, he had been so involved in visiting with his parents that he hadn't paid much attention to the view. Now, as he paused to study his surroundings, a flood of childhood memories washed over him.

Not much had changed since the last time he'd vacationed here, although he didn't recognize any of his fellow sunbathers. Several other "big noses," as the Koreans so affectionately called Americans, lay scattered about the beach. Compared to the handful of small-framed, darker-skinned natives who were busy digging clams from the freshly exposed shore at low tide, the pasty-white, flabby foreigners looked uncomfortably akin to beached whales.

His gaze rested on the form of a lone clam-digger skirting the foamy edge of rolling surf, and he laughed aloud when he recognized that the distant figure was Grace. With her pant legs rolled up around her knees and a pail dangling from her arm, she appeared childlike, unscathed by the eight-year passage of time since he'd been gone.

He left his gear and jogged toward her. As he drew closer, he cupped his hands around his mouth to form a makeshift megaphone before calling out her name.

"Grace!"

She turned to look in his direction, responding instantly by waving her free hand in a sweeping arch. He increased his speed from a jog to a run, and Grace waited for him to catch up to her. His quick sprint left him breathless and he grabbed his knees, gulping air before he attempted to speak.

"Need. . .some. . .help?" He tipped his head up to look at her, then he straightened to his full height as he took one final lung-filling swallow followed by a quick exhale. "I bet I can remember the best clam-digging spot on the beach. Follow me."

"The only help I need from you is your help in eating

them. You must be exhausted. I don't think you've gotten any sleep since you arrived at Taechon." Grace's brows knotted as she straightened and turned her head to gaze upward at him.

Without asking, he took the pail from her arm and motioned for her to follow him. "Well, the more we gather, the more I can help you eat. Come on. Let me show you where the clams hang out in this neighborhood. That little run invigorated me and I couldn't sleep now if I tried. You know, don't you, that they don't allow anyone to graduate from medical school until they've mastered the ability to function on little or no sleep?"

Grace, in typical Oriental fashion, fell into step two paces behind him. "Then that's just one more reason I could never be a doctor," she answered with a chuckle. "But, if you insist on helping me, then lead the way." They walked in comfortable silence past the bank of stairs going up to the chapel and on until the sand turned into a rocky stretch of shoreline, accessible only at low tide. A shallow, surf-carved cavern jutted into the overhanging cliff, and Philip briefly crouched in the shadows of the opening. When he straightened again, the sound of shellfish clanking against the sides of the metal pail echoed through the cave. Grace joined him in the harvest, and within minutes the bucket brimmed to overflowing.

"You can't carry this." Philip refused to allow Grace to take the pail from him. "Let me deliver this back to the cabin for you." He retraced their shoe-print trail but stopped at the cement stairs and plopped himself down on the bottom step, sinking the clam bucket into the soft sand between his feet.

"Dad told me you were in the chapel this morning." As Grace approached, he patted the place next to him. "I hope my ranting prayers didn't drive you off. You didn't have to leave. Actually, I am grateful for the chance to tell you about a couple of things that are really eating at me. I could use some advice, and you always had a level head about you. I'd appreciate your prayers, too. I couldn't bring myself to talk to Dad. For one thing, I don't want him to be disappointed if things don't work out like I'm thinking they will."

Instead of sitting beside him, Grace sank to her knees in the sand next to him.

"I don't know about the levelheaded part, but I'm honored that you would confide in me and I certainly will pray."

His eyes met hers for a fleeting second before she dropped her gaze and intently studied her folded hands. Her humble posture and sweet spirit filled him with a warm pleasure and sent a small smile pulling at the corners of his lips.

"Thanks, Grace. I knew I could count on you. Here's the deal. . ."

Philip raised one hand to rest it on the back of his neck, then straightened and drew a deep breath before he began to speak. "Jennifer's father is the chief of staff at a private hospital in San Francisco, and he's in charge of my residency. Dr. Anderson has really bent over backward to help me. He had to do some creative scheduling so that I could take enough time off to make this trip. Plus, he's already hinted strongly that he's put in a good word for me with a doctor friend of his and, apparently, I have an 'in' to become a junior partner as a general practitioner with him. Of course, the idea of settling down close to her folks thrills Jennifer to no end."

"Oh, that's wonderful—" Grace pressed her fingers to her lips.

"Well, yes and no. There's just one little glitch in this seemingly perfect plan. One big glitch, actually. . ."

He gulped another big breath before continuing.

"You see, for the past couple of months, I've been sensing that God is calling me to be a missionary doctor back here in Asia—either Korea or Japan. I already know the languages, and the need for doctors is so much greater here than back in the States. So, this trip to Korea involves more than introducing Jennifer to my folks. For weeks, I've been praying that God will use this trip to confirm or deny my missionary call, and the minute I set foot back in Korea, I felt an undeniable assurance that this is where God wants to use me."

A rush of excitement swept over him as he voiced, for the first time, his surety of God's call on his life to mission service. Yet, the dawning of a sadder revelation tempered the thrill of this one.

"I'm still waiting for the right moment to share all this with Jennifer. She's reacted so negatively to everything about Korea since we arrived. She seems downright miserable. I couldn't possibly spring on her now the idea of moving here permanently. Grace, you don't think God would call me to be a missionary without calling Jennifer, too, do you? The way I see it, a missionary's life is so tough, both the husband and wife need to know without a doubt that God is calling them to serve."

Grace's eyes widened more than he'd ever seen, and she gasped.

"*Paksanim,* do you mean to tell me that you haven't

discussed all this with Miss Jennifer? She needs to know immediately."

Before he could defend his position, Jennifer's voice cracked through his thoughts.

"Philip, what are you two talking about down there? What is it I need to know?"

He twisted around to see his mother, with Jennifer beside her, overshadowing them at the top of the stairs.

Jennifer perched her hands on her hips, and her eyes narrowed to a tight glare. "Are you keeping secrets from me?"

three

Eun-Me had already jumped to her feet and was brushing the sand from her britches when *Sahmonim* Woods called down to her, "Grace, why don't we leave these two alone? Sounds like they might need to chat awhile."

She responded with a quick nod.

"I'm praying for you, Philip," she murmured into his good ear as she retrieved the pail from between his feet and inched past him on her way up the stairs.

At the halfway point of her descent, Miss Jennifer breezed past Eun-Me without acknowledging her proffered "Excuse me" or extending the courtesy of the same.

"That poor dear," *Sahmonim* rasped in a loud whisper when Eun-Me fell into step behind her. "She's a beauty. That's for sure. But she's more skittery than a Mexican jumping bean."

"Yes, Ma'am," she replied, certain that she'd never seen a jumping bean of any nationality, but just as certain that the graphic description must fit Miss Jennifer perfectly.

The full pail swung awkwardly back and forth, forcing Eun-Me to clutch the metal handle with both hands in order to steady the load.

Sahmonim glanced at Eun-Me over her shoulder and slowed her pace. "Well, I can recall feeling mighty scared my first few days in Korea. We just need to give her some time to adjust. Don't you suppose?"

"Yes, Ma'am," Eun-Me parroted her previous response, but she wasn't at all confident that time would improve Miss Jennifer's caustic disposition.

"You don't think this little tiff they seem to be having will amount to anything serious, do you, Dear?"

"No, Ma'am. I hope not, Ma'am," she replied stoically, refusing to respond in any more detail to *Sahmonim's* not-so-subtle dig for information.

Fortunately, the genteel missionary respected Eun-Me's unspoken plea not to pry any further, and the two women fell silent for the remainder of their walk back to the cabin. Eun-Me seized the opportunity to pray in earnest for Philip, asking God to grant him the wisdom that she'd read about last night in the Book of James.

She shivered as a ripple of excitement swept over her at the thought that Philip might move back to Korea as a missionary. Even if she had to work hard not to expose her true feelings for him, she relished the idea of being near him frequently. Seeing his bright smile. Enjoying the pleasure of his company. But her tingles subsided as she considered the fact that Miss Jennifer would be ever present as well.

"Oh, *Hahnahnim,* give me a double portion of Your patience and understanding as far as Miss Jennifer is concerned," she breathed in concluding prayer when she and *Sahmonim* approached the cabin.

Philip's parents sequestered behind closed doors, and Eun-Me surmised that *Sahmonim* was explaining to her husband about this most recent and uncomfortable turn of events between their son and his future wife. Knowing her employers as well as she did, she knew that they would also spend time in concerted prayer.

When they reappeared in the living room an hour or so later, Eun-Me had busied herself with dusting and sweeping and tidying, chores that allowed her to watch and listen for the return of Philip and Miss Jennifer as well. Both *Sahmonim* and *Moksanim* thinly veiled their own nervous anxieties by dumping a new two thousand piece jigsaw puzzle onto the folding table they had set up in the far corner of the living room. Then, they lackadaisically sifted through the mountain of puzzle pieces in search of the straight-edged border ones.

Eun-Me dropped all pretenses of busyness when a duet of footsteps sounded on the back porch. Jennifer burst through the door first. With her head down and her hands hiding her face, she streaked across the living room, down the hallway, and into her bedroom, slamming the door behind her without bothering to remove her shoes.

Seconds later, Philip struggled through the back door. The assortment of beach gear he carried under one arm clattered to the floor when he stepped out of his beach flippers and kicked the door shut with the heel of his foot.

He clutched something in the balled fist of his right hand.

Walking over to his mother, he reached down and took hold of her wrist. Turning her palm up, he released that which he held in his grasp.

Eun-Me stared in disbelief at the sparkling object, which lay in *Sahmonim*'s outstretched hand. Just this morning at breakfast, she had admired the distinctive pearl-and-diamond engagement ring that graced Miss Jennifer's left hand. *Had he demanded its return? Or had she been the one to break their engagement?*

Her stomach sank at the guilt-pricking realization that her failure to keep her opinionated advice to herself was to blame for this row between Philip and Miss Jennifer. If she hadn't blurted her question at the beach loud enough for anyone to hear, all of this trouble could have been avoided. Philip knew his fiancée much better than she did, and he was surely sensitive enough to know the appropriate time to share with her the news of his missionary call.

When she caught sight of Philip's doleful frown, a fresh stab of remorse assaulted her thoughts. She swallowed hard to stifle her desire to comfort him.

Just because Philip had always confided in her when they were kids did not mean that she should offer her comments now. She told herself to forget the way things used to be. The years had changed their relationship, and it was now too presumptuous of her, an *ajumoni* with only an eighth-grade education, to tell a grown man with a doctor's degree what to do. Regardless of their past friendship, she no longer had the right to counsel, console, or admonish him —particularly concerning matters of romance.

As he addressed his mother, Eun-Me could no longer bear to look at Philip's face. She cared for him too much to see him in such pain. She fixed her gaze on the ring again.

"Please, Mom. Don't say anything. I'm not in the mood to discuss this now. I'll explain to both you and Dad as soon as I'm able." Philip's voice cracked with emotion when he folded his mother's fingers over the tiny golden band. "I need you to hold onto Grandma Carson's ring for safekeeping."

Moksanim rose from his seat, knocking several puzzle pieces to the floor with his shirtsleeve. "Don't you worry,

Son," he said as he moved to Philip's side and offered him a paternal pat on the back. "The two of you will work through this, whatever the problem may be."

Philip shook his head slowly from side to side. "I wish I could be certain of that. We'll see. But, if you'll excuse me, I think I need to be alone for awhile." Eun-Me watched Philip, his shoulders drooping, as he walked to the staircase. Grabbing the handrail, he looked as though he had to pull himself up the stairs.

When Philip had left the room, *Sahmonim* pinched the ring between her finger and thumb and held it up to the light. "You have no idea how hard it is for me not to order you to tell me what this is all about." Her smile held no joy as she lowered the ring and looked Eun-Me in the eye, but the weight of her statement came through, despite her pleasantness.

"Now, Mama. Stop your meddling." *Moksanim* sidled up to his wife and prodded her arm gently with his elbow. "Exercise the Lord's gift of patience in your life. You don't want Grace to break a confidence. I imagine that her ability to keep quiet is one of the reasons Philip shared his troubles with her. Our son will tell us the whole story in due time. What do you say we get out of this stifling cabin and go for a long walk? The mood is much too heavy in here. Grace, do you think you could rustle up a picnic lunch for Mama and me?"

Eun-Me did his bidding while they went in search of the wicker picnic basket in the storage area under the stairs. She had their lunch ready to pack when the elusive container finally appeared.

"I just peeked into Philip's room on my way downstairs,"

Sahmonim said when she came into the kitchen to retrieve the basket. "He's fallen asleep on top of his bed with his old scrapbook in his hands. I think we should let him sleep as long as he can. I'm awfully worried about him." She plopped a straw sun hat onto the unruly shock of her permed, sandy blond curls.

"Yes, Ma'am. I won't disturb him." Eun-Me laid two ripe persimmons on top of the *kimbap* lunch she had prepared and snapped the lid closed on the full picnic basket, before handing it over to *Moksanim*. "I suspect that Miss Jennifer is sleeping, also. I've not heard a sound come from her room in quite some time."

"Those poor dears. They'd both be more agreeable and their problems might be solved if the two of them could just get a good night's rest."

"That's your cure-all for everything that ails our world," *Moksanim* interjected. "Now, come along, my missionary mama. I'm sure Grace will appreciate a bit of peace and quiet so she can get her chores done."

❦

Grace stood at the sink washing dishes when Philip walked into the kitchen to get a drink. He paused, not wanting to interrupt her soft singing of his favorite Korean folk song, *"Ariyang."* When she finished the tune, he stepped up behind her and tapped her lightly on the shoulder.

"Eye-go!" she squeaked, making him regret sneaking up on her. She grabbed a cup towel from its hook and turned to face him as she dried her hands. Then, leaning back against the sink, she grasped the towel to her chest. "You scared me. I thought you were sleeping."

"Naw. I can't sleep in all this heat and sticky humidity.

And when I did manage to drift off, I had the most awful dream. Siberian tigers were chasing me all over the Korean countryside while I searched for Grandma Carson's lost ring. I woke up more exhausted than when I fell asleep." He pulled his hand from behind his back and offered her the paper bag he held.

"Sorry I scared you, but I wanted to give you these. I meant to give them to you yesterday when I arrived, but I forgot in all the hubbub."

She peered into the bag and then reached in and pulled out several packages of chocolate chips. "I remembered how much you loved chocolate chunk cookies as a kid, and I thought my mom could teach you how to make them using these chips, if you haven't already learned."

Philip jumped to sit on the countertop, leaving his feet to dangle several inches from the floor. "Speaking of Mom. . .are she and Dad around? I figured I might as well sit down and spell out this sticky situation to them."

He listened as Grace explained that his parents were out on a picnic but that they should be back soon. He dipped his head toward Jennifer's bedroom door and asked, "Have you seen or heard anything from her?"

"No. Miss Jennifer locked herself in her room and, other than a brief visit to the bathroom, she has not come out. She even refused to open the door to receive the lunch tray I prepared for her."

"That doesn't surprise me," he said with a sigh. "Well, go ahead and say, 'I told you so.'"

"I never should have let things go this far without telling Jennifer about my calling to missionary service. She really lashed into me this morning and said some pretty ugly things." Philip paused the nervous swaying of his feet and sighed, looking away from Grace to stare absently out the window to the dark trees.

"She said I tricked her. Even deliberately misled her about the possibility of going into private practice with her daddy's friend. She accused me of planning to marry her first, so that I could gain her father's financial backing, and then she'd have no choice but to let me drag her to the other side of the world to live in what she called 'a grass hut.' I tried to tell her that we could have a regular house just like Mom and Dad, but she refused to listen. She said she's not about to tag along in my shadow while I act like some kind of savior to the heathen. Then, she practically threw my engagement ring at me."

He heard Grace gasp, so he turned back to look at her. Her black eyes brimmed with tears of sympathy, and he struggled to maintain his own composure when he saw the compassion she felt for him. Jennifer might have rejected him, but he knew that he could always count on Grace to be a supportive and faithful friend.

She nodded. "So what are you going to do?"

"I've got no choice. I hate to spoil my folks' summer vacation by cutting it short, but Jennifer hates it here and can't seem to stand the thought of spending any more time with me. I guess I'm going to have to ask Dad if we can head back to Seoul tomorrow and see when the next freighter is scheduled to leave Inchon for San Francisco."

Rifle fire whistled through the air to signal the start of the daily military exercises. Just then, Jennifer stepped into the kitchen. Philip chuckled to consider the irony as he braced for some caustic remark from her. He imagined the crack of firearms outside served to warn him that mounting hostilities inside would soon explode again.

"Uh. . .Philip. I'd like to have a word with you." She tipped her head and looked down her nose at Grace as a not-so-subtle cue to her that her presence was not wanted. Grace muttered something about a matter that needed her attentions outside and left the kitchen before Philip could tell her that she didn't have to leave. He jumped down from his perch on the kitchen counter and waved his hand, indicating for Jennifer to take a seat on the davenport in the living room.

He sat facing her on the edge of the easy chair's cushion and, when he finally collected enough courage to look her in the eyes, she offered him a weak smile.

"I may have been too hasty when I gave you back the ring." As she spoke, she rubbed her tanned finger where the sun had tattooed a pale imprint of the missing engagement ring.

"My emotions got the best of me. Now that I've had a chance to cool down a bit, I've reconsidered things." She drew a deep breath and dropped her hands to her lap, then began to nervously smooth the wrinkles from her sundress.

"I know. . . I've done this a lot lately. . ." She stumbled on the words when she raised her eyes to look at him and began again. "I've done this a lot lately. B–b–but, I want to apologize." Her eyelids narrowed and made direct, unwavering eye contact.

When he didn't respond, she continued, her apology taking on a defensive tone.

"For starters, I admit, I overreacted a bit. Although you do realize, don't you, that you sprang some pretty big news on me? Everything here is so different and I've not had a chance to get used to things, and then I hear you saying you want to bring me here to live. I'm willing to pray about this missionary thing if you'll give me more time. After all, you have your residency to complete yet. A lot can happen between now and then. And I still think that maybe what you're sensing is really just happiness at being home and not a voice from God at all."

A tinge of enthusiasm lifted her voice as she continued speaking. "You know, if you really wanted to help the Korean people, you could be more effective by providing the funds to build a hospital or clinic and then financially supporting the staff. Think of the admiration you'd get from the medical community. And, with the help Daddy is promising, in no time at all you'll be generating an income that could easily handle that without putting the slightest crimp in our lifestyle."

Philip cleared his throat before he spoke. "First of all, Jennifer, if you're expecting me to return the ring to you right now, I'm afraid I can't do that. I gave the ring back to my mother for safekeeping since, originally, the ring belonged to her and to her mother before her. I figured I had no further use for the heirloom. Mom and Dad have gone for a picnic, so I couldn't give it back to you at the moment, even if I wanted to."

Jennifer's lips pursed into a thin, straight line of mounting animosity, and Philip measured his next words carefully.

"Frankly, I'm not sure I'm ready for you to wear the ring again." Jennifer's emerald eyes flashed at his words.

"I've had time to do a little thinking myself and I'm not ready to just kiss and make up. You said some pretty nasty things earlier. Obviously, you don't have much faith in my ability to make it on my own, without your daddy's help. And you've second-guessed my spiritual discernment as well." She shook her head back and forth, and he rushed to finish his speech before she could interrupt.

"If your apology still stands, then I accept it and you are forgiven. In hindsight, I realize I should have shared with you as soon as I began to sense a mission call. So, for that, I apologize to you as well. But, in light of your response today, I was right to worry about your reaction. I think we really need to give this time and talk things through before we rush back into making wedding plans."

Jennifer rose to her feet to loom over him and the icy glare she gave him erased all hints of her earlier penitence. "So, tell me, Philip, what am I supposed to do in the meantime? Sit around in this miserable place and wait for you to think about it some more?" She tapped her foot and crossed her arms. "Just how long do you plan to punish me and make me wait?"

White-hot anger pounded at his temples at her unpremeditated description of his homeland. He clinched his jaw in a futile attempt to choke back his indignation.

"If you find Korea to be such a miserable place, then it's because you have made it so. The only thing miserable around here that I can see is the misery you've brought." Philip pushed off the arms of the easy chair and stood to look down on Jennifer.

"If, in all honesty, you think I could slough off God's call on my life simply by throwing money at a worthy cause, then you don't have a clue about the true meaning of Christian service. I would be happier living here in abject poverty and all alone, even in that grass hut, which you speak of with such disdain, than living a life of luxury with some spoiled and selfish socialite." His voice escalated with each incensed word. "I won't be bullied into a hurried decision that I'll regret the rest of my life. Do you understand?"

Yet, even in his anger, Philip sensed that he had settled the issue about his call once and for all. Nothing else—no one else—would stop him from following the Lord's leading in his life. If that meant serving alone, then so be it. Whatever the cost, he would follow God's leading in his life and serve Him.

A sudden peace washed over him, supplanting his exasperation with Jennifer. He exhaled his tension in a puff of breath and his shoulders relaxed. However, Jennifer's face appeared almost purple in rage at his blunt scorn, and she lashed back at him with fury.

"A spoiled and selfish socialite, huh? Well, you sure didn't seem to feel that way just a few days ago. I didn't know I'd promised to marry such a pompous, pious saint. You can keep your cheap old engagement ring. I wouldn't marry you if you were the last man on earth."

Her lack of originality struck a strange cord of humor in Philip as she continued her diatribe.

"Remember, when you get back to San Francisco you still have a three-year residency program to complete under Daddy's supervision. I'm certain you'll come to regret all this sooner or later. But when that day comes, don't come crawling back to me begging for forgiveness."

She tilted her chin into the air and stomped her foot to punctuate her final demand. "How soon can I get out of here? I want to go home."

A gloomy darkness overshadowed the room, and Philip glanced out the open window to see a bank of murky clouds moving across the late afternoon sun. "First, let me say that I already regret getting so mad at you."

She replied with a low, "Hurmph," but he continued on.

"I shouldn't have let my emotions take over like that. You and I both know that I'm not given to such outbursts, but I still need to offer you an apology. It's not my place to judge you and I wish I could take back that 'spoiled and selfish' remark." He stared at Jennifer until she returned his gaze.

"But the more we talk, the more I realize, you and I aren't meant for one another. I don't think you could ever be happy living so far away from your folks, and I am more convinced than ever that God is calling me here."

The racket of war games had stopped, replaced by an eerie, death-quiet serenity. Philip's words sliced through the stillness.

"I'm sorry we had to come all this way to make such an unpleasant discovery, but I promise to do whatever I can to get you back home to San Francisco immediately. As soon as Dad comes in, I'll speak to him about our returning to Seoul tomorrow." He could see tears threatening to spill down her cheeks and a welling pity overtook him.

"Jennifer—" He wavered, then decided to add one last thought. "Let's try to make this unpleasant situation as easy on one another as possible. What do you say, we part company on friendly terms rather than as enemies?"

Jennifer stared at him for several long seconds and when she finally did respond, she ignored his proposal altogether.

"This is awkward, I know. However, I need to ask you for another dose of that sedative. I thought I'd brought plenty of my own when we left San Francisco, but I've run out."

Droplets of perspiration beaded across her upper lip, and she swiped a hand brusquely over her mouth before she continued.

"My mother knew how nervous I was about making this trip and she had shared a few of her pills with me to help calm my nerves. However, I've had such trouble sleeping and my nerves have given me such a terrible time these past couple of months, especially these last two weeks, that I've used up my supply. Would you kindly share just a couple more?"

The impact of her confession caused his jaw to drop in disbelief. "Do you realize what you've done, Jennifer? You've developed a dependency on those sedatives. No wonder your moods have seesawed so. I'm sorry, but I can't let you have anymore. You'll have a rough few days until the medicine is out of your system, but I'll try to help you all I can." He reached out to lay a hand on her shoulder, but she yanked away and glowered at him through slitted eyes.

"How ridiculous. I'm not addicted to any drugs. They were only mild sedatives. My dad's a doctor, for goodness sake. He would never have given my mother anything harmful. And another thing: Whether or not I've had my nerve pills won't change my decision not to marry you."

She signaled her retreat by tossing her hair out of her face in a quick jerk and spinning away from him. "I'll be in my room if you find a shred of decency within you and decide to give me those pills." She tromped down the hall on bare feet as she called out over her shoulder, "Just stay as far away from me as possible until I can get out of here."

❦

Sunday, June 25, 1950

Eun-Me laid on her *yoh* listening to the early morning cricket songs long before the alarm clock rang. Philip and the events of yesterday so filled her thoughts that her mind refused to rest. She made a mental list in preparation for their hasty departure, for they would all be returning to Seoul after the worship service today. Miss Jennifer was going back to America where she belonged.

After dinner, Philip had insisted on Eun-Me's presence when he explained to his parents about his call to be a missionary, then he filled in the blanks concerning his resulting quarrel and breakup with Miss Jennifer. For Philip's sake, Eun-Me was sorry that things weren't working out between the two of them. Moreover, she pitied Miss Jennifer's nervous condition. But she had to squelch a flash of pleasure at the thought that the American would soon be gone.

Philip did seem to be handling the situation well, however. Much better than Miss Jennifer, who had locked herself in her room throughout the remainder of the evening. Even *Sahmonim* couldn't coax her out.

Throwing back the heavy quilt, Eun-Me slid her feet onto the hard linoleum and stood. To remain in bed and fret about all that needed to be done was simply a waste of time, regardless of the hour. Since they would all worship together later this morning, she wouldn't be going out for dawn prayers, but if she worked quietly, she could use this time to get a good start on packing things away in the cabin.

She felt her way through the dark room until she found

the light switch and flipped it on. She stood still and blinked away the ensuing temporary blindness until her eyes adjusted to the stark, bright light, then she slipped into her shirtwaist dress. Before beginning the work she knew must be done in preparation for them to leave, she quickly rolled up her *yoh* and tucked it neatly under a shelf of canned goods that she and *Sahmonim* had put up last year. With all around her silent, she chuckled quietly to herself with the knowledge that she wouldn't have to wait in line for the bathroom at this time of day.

Toothbrush in hand, she began her journey to the bathroom, but her feet skidded to a halt in the open doorway. Philip, already dressed in khaki slacks and a white oxford shirt, sat crouched on the davenport with his transistor radio held close to his good ear. Her heart went out to him. He must still be having a hard time sleeping because of the time differences between America and Korea, or perhaps because of worry over Miss Jennifer.

She tried to smile, knowing she'd surprised him, but a second glance showed more than mere surprise in his eyes. Eun-Me laid her toothbrush on the kitchen counter and moved toward Philip as he rose, still clutching his radio, to meet her halfway across the room.

His brow knotted, and his face was strangely pale, even for an anemic-looking American. His voice came out as barely a whisper. "From what I can make out between my rusty Korean and all this static, Communist forces from the north invaded Seoul less than an hour or so ago. The city is under attack."

four

Eun-Me's knees buckled and she grabbed hold of the dining table to steady herself. "How could this be? All the reports lately seemed to be saying that the threat of invasion appeared minimal."

Philip pulled a chair out from the table and motioned for her to sit. Accepting the offered seat, she rested her elbows on the table and briefly buried her face in her hands. When she dropped her hands into a fist on her lap and looked up at Philip again, he had pulled a chair away from the table and sat facing her, backward in his seat and straddling the ladder-back.

"Apparently, the Communists took advantage of that element of surprise. Let's hope and pray that our forces repel them quickly and send them packing back up north." He set the transistor radio between them on the table and Eun-Me's gaze traveled back and forth between Philip and the squawking, barking black box. The frantic voice crackling over the airwaves reported tanks and artillery plowing at an alarming and steady rate into the city north of the Han River.

"Oh, Philip, we live north of the Han." She fired a rapid volley of questions at him without giving him an opportunity to respond. "Do you suppose they've reached our *dong?* What are we going to do? Should we waken the others and prepare to evacuate?"

Philip raised his palms to her and shook his head. "We shouldn't overreact just yet, Grace. You know how news reports tend to exaggerate these rumors of war. This may turn out to be nothing more than another skirmish along the 38th parallel."

Eun-Me tried to relax at his calming tone.

"I'll go and roust my folks here in a minute to get their advice. Dad's usually awake by now, anyway. However, I do *not* think we should disturb her." He jerked his head in the direction of Jennifer's bedroom. "There's no telling how she's going to react to this news. This certainly puts a kink in her plans to leave. The chances aren't looking too good that we'll be going back to Seoul today."

Philip gently encased her hand in his grasp. "Whatever happens, Grace, I'm confident that the Lord is going to watch over us. And I promise to do my best to take care of you."

Eun-Me couldn't speak through her emotion-clogged throat, so she only nodded. Philip's touch as he held her hand enabled her to push aside the fearful threat of impending war for a few seconds.

He gave her hand a final, gentle squeeze before releasing his grip and rising from his seat. As he passed behind her, he rested his hand on her shoulder. "Now, I'd better go see about waking Mom and Dad. If you don't mind, I think we'd better turn off the radio to preserve the batteries. I've just got a couple of extras, and who knows when or if we'll be able to buy more. I don't imagine they'll be able to confirm or deny these invasion reports until daylight, anyway."

Eun-Me also stood and reclaimed her toothbrush from the kitchen counter, her hand still warm from Philip's touch. "Go ahead and switch it off. I need to finish getting ready. Then I'll start cooking breakfast right away."

When Philip headed for the stairs, Eun-Me hurried to the bathroom and, within minutes, had returned to the kitchen to start breakfast. Once the rice came to a boil on the stove, she turned the fire down to maintain a slow simmer and began to rummage through the top drawer for a pencil and small notepad.

She jotted down a list of things to do in the event that they were forced to flee. Most of her list dealt with the preparation of food that they could carry and eat easily in the car. Eun-Me chewed on the end of her pencil and looked out the kitchen window while she thought. A light drizzle dripped from the early morning sky, filtering the first light of day.

At the sound of footsteps descending the stairs, Eun-Me left her list-making and set out a traditional Korean breakfast for the Woods family. She would wait until Miss Jennifer emerged from her room before preparing a plate of fried eggs and ham for the sullen guest.

As Philip and his parents took their seats at the dining table, their demeanor mirrored the gravity of the early morning news. They ate in silence while Eun-Me tended to their needs.

After breakfast, *Sahmonim* volunteered to help Eun-Me tackle the items on her "To Do" list. They started by baking a batch of cookies using the chocolate chips that Philip had brought from America. They worked for an hour or so while Philip and his father moved to the living room to huddle over the radio.

"Mama, Grace," *Moksanim* called to them from the living room, "the news from Seoul sounds grave. I think we should all gather around and kneel for a season of prayer. I doubt if we'll be having church services in the chapel in light of these developments, but I need to spend some time talking to the Lord."

Eun-Me and *Sahmonim* left the kitchen and joined Philip and his father in the living room. They all dropped to their knees on the floor around the coffee table. *Moksanim* led, and then each one took a turn praying aloud.

While Philip prayed, Eun-Me took comfort from the familiar manner in which he spoke to the Lord. Obviously, prayer was not just a ritual for him, but communication with a close Friend. Her admiration for him grew as he concluded his prayer with a plea that Jennifer would find happiness.

When he asked for divine help in getting Jennifer safely and quickly back to San Francisco, Eun-Me grimaced with guilt. Philip expressed compassion for the woman who had hurt and rejected him. Her own thoughts and concerns had centered on how today's events might affect her life alone.

She'd given little or no consideration to how an enemy invasion might terrify Miss Jennifer. Instead, she viewed her as a bother. A burden. A hindrance should they need to flee to safety. If Philip could demonstrate such a Christlike attitude, despite a broken heart, surely she could find it within herself to do likewise. In quiet petition, she vowed to be more loving and kind.

Eun-Me waited to pray aloud until each of the others had taken a turn. She couldn't hold back her tears as she abandoned her use of English and poured out her heart to the Lord in her native Korean. She echoed the Woodses' previous prayers, expressing her fear at the thought of war. She cried out, questioning how it could be that their own countrymen were waging battle against them. She pleaded for peace and the Lord's protection over them, as well as safety for their friends and church family back home in Seoul. She begged for a quick end to the fighting.

Despite the harsh realities of war that now stared them in the face, her panic dissipated and a calmness overtook her while she prayed. She sensed God's undeniable presence and His peace in their midst.

As *Moksanim* pronounced the final "Amen," and they stood to their feet, the wild clanging of a bell pierced the early morning air. "Someone's sounding the alarm, calling us all to gather for an emergency meeting," he said, pushing back from the table and rising to his feet. "We need to go to the chapel right away. Mama, you'd better get Jennifer up. She needs to be in on all this."

But before *Sahmonim* could move, Miss Jennifer opened the door to her bedroom and stepped into the hall. She wore the same powder blue shift she'd been wearing yesterday, but deep wrinkles now creased the dress.

"Is this Sunday morning bell ringing another Korean custom that Dr. Woods forgot to tell me about, or is something going on?" She looked from *Moksanim* to *Sahmonim*, then to Eun-Me, with deliberate care not to look in the direction of Philip. *Sahmonim* rushed over and gave the willowy blond a quick hug.

"Dear, the bell is used to summon everyone on the compound. We're to gather at the chapel as soon as possible. We didn't want to alarm you until we'd learned more of the details, but by all indications, Communist forces from the north invaded Seoul around four o'clock this morning."

Jennifer raked her hair from her face with a trembling hand, and Eun-Me watched as her fair skin paled to an ashen gray.

"But I've got to get home. Philip, what have you gotten me into? My nerves can't handle this." Her words hissed with venom as she glared at him through narrowed eyes. "Daddy will hold you personally responsible if anything happens to—"

"My son can't be held responsible for acts of war, Miss Anderson." *Moksanim* interrupted her before she could finish her threat. He walked across the room and put his arm around his wife's shoulder as she stood next to Jennifer. His size alone gave him an air of authority, but never in all the years that Eun-Me had known *Moksanim* Woods had she heard him speak in such a stern manner. His words were almost harsh.

"Situations like this require full cooperation from all of us, not criticism. Please bear this in mind. I promise you that we'll do our very best to see that you are safely delivered home. Right now, all of us—including you—need to get over to the chapel and discuss this crisis with the others. I hope I've made myself clear. Come along, Mama. Let's go."

Jennifer cowered as though she'd been slapped and lagged behind the others as they put on their shoes and headed down the path to the chapel.

❦

Philip led their little entourage into the chapel, where a tense hush settled over the group of foreigners already assembled. As his parents, Grace, and Jennifer passed by him to take their seats, a solemn-faced, rigid figure in a U.S. military uniform approached him with his hand outstretched.

"Woods, Russell Barnard here. It's unfortunate that we meet again under such tenuous circumstances, but I'm pleased to see you after so many years. Have you gotten word of the Communist invasion?"

He pumped the soldier's hand up and down. "Rusty, glad you introduced yourself. I would have never recognized you in that uniform. I remember you as that scruffy, red-headed shortstop on our mission school baseball team. Guess we've both changed a bit since then." Philip noticed the GI's parents sitting on the front row, and he nodded to them in greeting when they looked his way. "I didn't realize you and your folks were here."

Turning back to the lieutenant, he lowered his voice to a near whisper. "But, to answer your question, yes. I've had my radio on most of the morning, trying to catch the reports. As a member of the armed forces, do you have any inside information that the radio announcers aren't telling us?" He fell into step beside the lanky soldier and together they made their way to the front.

"I'll be sharing with the rest of the group here in a minute, but I fear the worst. I am currently assigned to the Korean Liaison Office, Far East Command, in Japan, and I just happened to be taking a two-week leave to vacation here in Taechon with my folks. I'm going to evacuate the three of us back to Japan on the first military transport we can catch. Until this crisis blows over, I'd advise you to do the same. We're leaving for Kimpo right away in hopes that we can beat the Communists there." The soldier's advice sounded more like a command than a suggestion.

"Unfortunately, we don't have the connections or access to military transportation that you do, and I'd be a little nervous about heading toward the action, even if I did. But I need to find some way to get my friend here back to America." He made a cursory nod toward Jennifer, who sat scowling, with her arms folded, in the pew behind his parents. His heart warmed to see that Grace had moved to sit beside his poor, pathetic ex-fiancée.

"Maybe someone among the group will have a suggestion," he added, shrugging his shoulders.

"I wish I could help you out, but my hands are tied. However, if you can find your way to the US-KMAG compound at the Daejon Air Field, they should help you to safety, if need be."

Philip scrunched his forehead in bewilderment. "That's quite an acronym. What does it mean?"

"We've taken to calling it 'K-mag' for short. Stands for our American Army's Korean Military Assistance and Advisory Group," Lieutenant Barnard said as he stepped up onto the platform. "They are designated as a gathering point and would be responsible for the task of evacuating our American refugees, should the situation warrant that. I'll be happy to give you directions after the meeting." Philip took the cue to excuse himself and took a seat next to his father as Rusty addressed the group.

"Well, I believe everyone's assembled. Let's get this meeting under way. Since I rang the bell, I'll assume the responsibility of serving as the unofficial chair—unless someone objects."

Philip's childhood schoolmate briefed the group on the latest accounts of the invasion. In conclusion, he reiterated his earlier statement he'd made privately to Philip—that everyone should consider leaving Taechon as soon as possible and head south, away from the advancing troops. He pointed out that enemy forces could traverse the distance from the capital city to Taechon in a matter of hours.

As the gravity of the situation unfolded, a woman seated on the front row with her family raised her hand for attention, then stood. "My name is Helen Carroll, and my husband, Tim, and I and our two boys, Michael and Caleb—" She nodded in their direction while she spoke. "We arrived in Korea six months ago to serve as independent missionaries. We are living in Seoul until we finish language school and brought our sons down here on the train for a long weekend. . ."

Her voice cracked with emotion, and she covered her mouth with her hand to stifle a sob. She regained her composure after a couple of deep breaths and continued. "We're out here in the middle of the boondocks. Literally." She dabbed at her cheeks with a handkerchief and patted the back of her young son, who had come to her side and wrapped his arms around her legs. The older of the two boys, whom Philip guessed to be about six years old, sat at stoic attention on the other side of his father, but he brusquely swiped away his own tears with the back of his hand at the sight of his mother weeping.

"The trains run sporadically and the schedules are chaotic at the best of times. How do you propose that we get to this evacuation place you suggested? We don't have a satchel full of money to bribe our way to safety." She lowered herself back into her seat and pulled her child onto her lap. Her husband pulled her close, and she buried her head into his shoulder.

Philip's dad stood and moved toward the front. "First of

all, let me say thank you to Lieutenant Barnard for his report."

The GI left the podium and sat on the front row, yielding the floor to the veteran missionary.

"And, Ma'am—" He addressed Mrs. Carroll directly, but his words were meant for the entire assembly. "I'm committed to seeing that everyone here reaches a safe haven. I have a car and, if we have to, we'll cram into it like sardines." He looked back and forth over the audience. "How many here would want to go with us in our Studebaker to Daejon?"

A show of hands indicated seven people, not counting the Woods family group. Included in that number were Richard Spencer, the unmarried missionary professor from their own mission, and Frank and Gloria Taylor, career missionaries with the OMA mission board, as well as the four members of the Carroll family.

Philip's dad drew a deep breath and then released a low whistle through his clenched teeth. "That'd make twelve of us in a two-door sedan. A tight squeeze, even for sardines. Perhaps we men should go into town and at least check on the train schedules. We won't know unless we try. Doesn't Jesus teach us that we have not because we ask not?"

While his dad arranged a meeting time and place with the other men for their trip to town, Philip felt a tap on his shoulder. He twisted around in his seat to see Jennifer, her face shrouded in seriousness. "I need to speak to you and your father," she rasped into his right ear. "Right away. Before you go to town."

He studied her green eyes, searching for clues to explain

her request, praying that she didn't have any other bomb-shell surprises to drop on them.

"All right," he whispered back at her, "I'll meet you at the cabin before we head into town, but we'll have to make it quick. I have to get directions to the Daejon evac-uation center from Rusty before we go, and Dad wants to leave for the station in ten minutes or so."

"A minute is all I need."

As Jennifer slid back into her seat, Philip stole a quick glance at Grace sitting next to her. The two women pro-vided a startling study in contrast. One short, the other tall. One blond and fair, the other black-haired and olive-skinned. One calm, the other a nervous wreck. Yet, while the physical differences were stark, he marveled at the spirit and attitude differences even more. When surrounded by the affluence and high society of San Francisco, he'd been blind to Jennifer's self-consuming and superficial ways. But now, compared to Grace, those negative traits glared apparent.

The cadence of his heartbeat quickened to see Grace, with her head bowed, hands folded in her lap, and her lips moving in silent prayer. He admired her quiet strength and tender spirit. She owned nothing. She had no one with whom she could share life. She'd lost everyone near and dear to her. By all rights, she could be bitter and disillu-sioned. Yet, she was an example of trust. Sweetness. Kind-ness. Love.

Philip jolted out of his reverie when his mother tapped him on the knee. "If you will let me by, I will escort the girls back to the cabin so we can get right to the work of packing."

"Oh, sure. I'll be coming right behind you. I just need to get those directions from Rusty." He followed his mother into the aisle, where they headed in opposite directions. While the women left the chapel, he joined his dad at the front and waited for the cluster of people around Rusty to leave. When they were finally able to approach the GI, he sketched a simple map for them on the back of a piece of scrap paper, and they wished each other well as they parted company.

On the way back to the cabin, Philip told his father about Jennifer's request to speak with them, but he didn't expect to find her waiting on the back steps when they approached. Clutching something in her hand, she ran toward them while they were still several yards away.

The firs dripped with the residue of the morning's light rain, and the rising summer heat left the air heavy and uncomfortable to breathe. "Reverend Woods. I had hoped for just the right moment to make a special presentation of this gift to you, but this crisis supersedes such ceremony. My daddy wanted you to have this for your mission work." She handed him a black velvet pouch, and Philip looked over his dad's shoulder as he unsnapped the fastener to reveal a one-inch stack of crisp and new U.S. currency.

"That Mrs. Carroll said something about not having a satchel full of money and, well, I figured you might be short on cash, too. If you need to use this three thousand dollars to get us out of here, I'm sure Daddy will reimburse you for any expenses you incur in getting me home."

Never had Philip seen so much cash altogether in one place. He felt rather certain that his dad hadn't either, for his voice cracked when he spoke. "I hardly know what to say. A mere 'thank you' isn't nearly sufficient. Your father is more than generous, Miss Anderson. We will certainly take great care to use this gift wisely."

"Daddy considers himself quite the philanthropist. He does this kind of thing all the time. I only hope there's enough to get me home."

Grace could live for more than several years on the tithe of this amount. How sheltered Jennifer's life must have been if she didn't realize just how far these funds would go or comprehend the risk of carrying so much money, even without the threat of war. She could practically charter her own freighter to carry her to San Francisco with the money in that pouch. Then, again, cash might prove worthless in protecting them from the adversaries and adversities they might face in the days ahead.

Despite the fact that Jennifer had offered the gift, in part, to save her own skin, Philip knew that her father was a truly kind and generous man. A twinge of regret passed through his thoughts when he considered the financial support he could provide to the mission effort if he followed Jennifer's advice and stayed in the States to practice medicine. If he patched things up with her and married into the Anderson family, he had no doubt that this cash gift would be just the tip of the iceberg when it came to her father's generosity. With the doctor's influential backing, he could be generating a hefty income of his own within no time.

Yet, he sensed a growing assurance that God had called him to be a missionary. He couldn't turn his back on his call now, no matter how much the decision cost him. And since their "discussions" and subsequent breakup yesterday, he realized he would forever regret marrying Jennifer.

He only prayed that there would still be a place for him to serve in Korea at the end of his residency program. For, although he had announced to Grace his willingness to live and work in either Korea or Japan, he struggled with lingering bitterness toward the Japanese. He had wrestled against the temptation to be glad that the Korean aggressors, and his personal tormentors, had been humbled and defeated in the recent world war. While the people of Japan desperately needed the gospel message, he wasn't sure he was up to such a task. God still needed to do a mighty work in his life concerning his animosity toward the Japanese. The most he could muster was a willingness to be willing for a change in his prejudiced heart.

He felt a nudge and looked to see his dad holding out the velvet pouch for him to take. "Son, I'd feel better if you were to take half of this. The thought of carrying so much cash scares me, but I don't think we have a choice. I think I'll ask Eun-Me to sew a secret pocket into my pant leg. You might want to consider doing the same."

He could picture Grace, sitting cross-legged on the floor of the living room, meticulously stitching money into his slacks. With the thought, he couldn't help but compare the two women once more. He swallowed against the welling emotion the comparison brought. While he was grateful for the funds, he realized that Jennifer's idea of being of service to others was to throw her money around. Her talent in sewing was limited to what she could do with a safety pin. But Grace. Grace lived to serve the needs of others. She found joy in being useful. Such assets could prove to be more valuable than cash in the end.

"The hidden compartments will have to wait until this

evening." Philip rushed to divvy up his portion of the funds into three bundles and crammed them into the pockets of his roomy trousers. "Here come the other men. We need to head into town. If you'll toss me the keys to the Stude-baker, I'll start the engine. Oh, and Jennifer, thanks again."

She shrugged off his gratitude and began to walk back to the cabin. "No need to thank me. I had nothing to do with it other than to make the delivery, and I promised Daddy that I would."

❧

When the screen door slammed, Eun-Me looked up from her job of packing away the beach and picnic gear in the storage closet under the stairs to see Jennifer crossing from the living room to the kitchen. She grimaced at the sight of the American wearing shoes on the spotless linoleum floor that she had worked so hard to clean. Yet, she gave Jennifer the benefit of the doubt by assuming that she simply wasn't accustomed to removing her shoes at the door and hadn't stopped to think. Jennifer came up alongside *Sah-monim* as she stood at the counter, wrapping in waxed paper the cookies they had made.

"Mrs. Woods, if you're finished looking through my bridal catalogues and magazines, I ought to pack them away. Even though it appears that I won't be needing them anytime soon, several of my sorority sisters are getting married within the year, so I might as well take them back home and give them away. Hopefully, someone else can make good use of them." The inference to the recent breakup charged the air with uneasiness.

"Certainly, Dear. Go ahead and take them. But if we're forced to cram twelve people into our car, I doubt that we'll have room for suitcases and the like. You might need to pack a separate, smaller bag with just a change or two of clothes and the bare necessities. I'll loan you my canvas shopping bag to use if you'd like."

The idea seemed to shock Jennifer even more than the announcement of the Communist invasion. "I can't leave my suitcase behind. I bought a whole new summer wardrobe for this trip. Who knows if or when my things would ever make it back to San Francisco should I be forced to abandon my luggage here? I'll get Philip to strap it to the top of the car with rope. Grace, while you're digging around under the stairs, find a length of rope for us to use."

"We'll leave that to the men to decide." A hint of irritation laced *Sahmonim's* voice. "Why don't you run along and get your things together? We may have to leave at a moment's notice, so we need to be prepared."

Eun-Me latched the hook on the storage cabinet and rose to her feet. Every encounter she had with Miss Jennifer left her in need of fresh air. She moved over to the entryway and gathered up the rug in order to carry it outside and shake out the sand. Pushing the front screen door open with her hip, she stepped onto the cement step. Then, closing her eyes and turning her head to one side, she released the dust from the rug with a flick of her wrists.

The blare of a horn made her jump, and she opened her eyes to see a battered, open-bed military truck pulling into the compound ahead of the Woodses' car. Philip waved to her from behind the steering wheel. Despite the seriousness of their circumstance, she couldn't stop the ripples of joy that made her smile at the sight of him, and a silly grin split his face in return.

She dropped the rug by the door and ran to the passenger side of the truck. When it screeched to a halt, she laid her hands across the open window frame and stood on her tiptoes to peer across the truck's cab at Philip. *Moksanim* Woods brought his sedan to a stop behind the truck. He and his companions piled out of the car, but they continued in deep discussion, paying no attention to Philip or Eun-Me.

"Here is your knight in shining armor, come to rescue the damsel in distress astride his trusty steed."

She didn't really understand what he was saying, but she laughed anyway. "Where did you get this?"

"As we feared, the train schedules have been thrown into total chaos. So, Dad coerced the local police chief into selling us this pile of junk. He vowed that it'd make the trip to Daejon without a breakdown or he'd give us our money back. Of course, we'll have to find him first. But the tires are good as new, and we didn't see any other options, so we thought we'd take the chance."

Eun-Me shot a glance behind the cab to the flatbed. "Miss Jennifer will be happy to hear that she can carry her suitcase along."

"Miss Jennifer better think again if she thinks I'm going to lug that trunk of hers all over the Korean countryside. I think we need to establish some ground rules before we set out on this journey. And rule number one is, each one must carry their own gear."

"Then I suppose I should be thankful that all I own fits nicely in a knapsack." The prospect of their imminent departure sobered her, and she looked at the men standing next to the car behind them.

"Are we leaving right away?"

"No. We plan to set out at first light tomorrow morning. We don't want to be caught out in the middle of nowhere after dark. We men will each take a turn as a lookout through the night and if anything suspicious occurs, we'll ring the chapel bell. In the meantime, though, Dad and I have a little sewing project that requires your experienced hand. Can you scrounge up a needle and thread?"

five

When he had finished changing his clothes, Philip stepped out of the bathroom and looked down at the hem of his trousers. "You did a great job, Grace. Even I wouldn't know there were secret pockets along the cuff if I hadn't watched you sew them in."

She sat on the floor beside the living room coffee table with her legs crossed, already stitching a similar pocket into the lining of his dad's pant leg. He found himself alone in the room with her. Jennifer, pleading a headache, had asked for a dinner tray in her room, and his parents had excused themselves right after the meal so that they could finish packing and rest up in preparation for the coming journey.

"There's nothing to this kind of handwork. I started mending our family's clothes when I was seven years old." She lowered her sewing to her lap, and her face lit up with a wide smile as she looked up at him.

When they were kids, he had always teased her about her eyes disappearing when she smiled, and now her almond-shaped eyes reduced to mere slits as she grinned. The vision and associated memory filled him with warm pleasure. It was good to see his old friend again.

He sat facing her in the easy chair and pulled his leg up by the ankle onto his other knee. "Knowing that rough-house brother of yours, I imagine Eun-Soo did his part in making you an expert seamstress." He picked a stray thread from his pants and balled it between his fingers, then flicked it into the air.

"I never minded." Eun-Me's smile faded to a pensive pout, and she shook her head slowly from side to side. "He always treated me better than any little sister deserved. Unlike most *oh-pah,* my brother always showed me respect—something most Korean men won't do for any woman, let alone a younger sister. I've got you to thank for that."

He raised a hand in protest and leaned toward her to emphasize his words. "His kindness to you isn't something I can take the credit for. He really loved you, you know. And he felt such a responsibility to look after you and your *omma* when *Moksanim* Cho was killed. He had a kind heart. This world needs more men like him. I really miss the guy."

"Me, too. But I never had a doubt about his faith or his salvation, and I'm sure he and my parents are enjoying the rewards of heaven right now."

Her features softened. Her eyes took on a pensive, unfocused glaze. And, although she looked straight at him, he felt that her spirit was far away.

"I often cry to think that I'm all that's left of our family." She spoke so softly that he had to tilt toward her with his good ear to catch her words. "I feel like just a piece of scrap. The salvage. A remnant of the rich heritage my family left to me. I'll never be able to pass that heritage on to another generation. I'm uneducated and unmarriageable. What good am I?"

The question stunned him. Sweet-spirited Grace personified beauty and ability and goodness. He didn't understand how she could possibly feel so insecure. Women would always be a mystery to him. He'd never once known Jennifer to question her self-worth, yet Grace had so many more gifts and talents to offer than Jennifer.

He planted both feet on the floor in front of him and leaned forward until his eyes were mere inches from hers. "You can't let yourself think like that. I can't honestly say that I understand why God would allow you to endure the suffering you have had to face in your lifetime. I can't fathom why He would take your family from you and leave you orphaned. However, I do know that you remain here on earth for a reason. You are a constant blessing to my family —for what that's worth. But beyond that, God has a special plan for you. When you start to feel overwhelmed and in-significant, remember the potential of a tiny mustard seed."

She nodded, yet he had the strong impression that he hadn't gotten through to her. He had to find some way to convince her that he wasn't just offering platitudes. He pushed himself off at his knees and stood to loom over her.

"Hey, I drew the first shift of the night watch duty. Why don't you come along with me and catch the sunset on the ocean one last time before we leave? If the war situation continues to escalate, we may not have another opportunity like this for a good long time."

And he may not have the chance to speak with her alone for a good long time, either, but he kept this thought to himself.

❧

Eun-Me fumbled with her sewing as she picked it up and returned her full attention to her work. Again, she had let herself get carried away with her loose tongue and had said more than she should have. She could feel the burn of her cheeks, and she kept her head down as she replied. "I'd like to, but I have to finish this and I still have several other jobs to do." She knew Philip was watching her, but she refused to look his way.

"I don't want to keep you from your work, but I wish you'd reconsider. My guard shift doesn't start for awhile, so if you change your mind, come get me. I'll be outside checking the oil on the truck."

She jabbed her needle into the stiff fabric of the pant leg, pricking her finger and drawing a bead of blood. As she sucked on the puncture wound, she chided herself for not refusing outright Philip's offer for a sunset walk on the beach. At the risk of further vulnerability, she dared not trust herself to be alone with him.

With just a raised eyebrow or a show of concern, he had the power to draw the most intimate of disclosures from her. She couldn't allow herself to invest any more emotionally. She had already said far too much. Revealed too many of her private thoughts. Exposed feelings too tender. She possessed enough good sense to know that nothing could ever develop between the two of them. They were worlds apart in every way. If she allowed their relationship to progress any further, she merely raised her risk of heartbreak.

At all costs, she had to guard her heart.

When she had finished her sewing, she locked herself in the bathroom and hand-washed her work clothes, hanging them to dry over the tub so that she could wear them tomorrow. Before exiting, she cracked the door open a sliver and made certain that she was not going to face Philip when she stepped into the open area of the kitchen and living room.

❦
Monday, June 26, 1950

Eun-Me set her kerchief-tied bundle on top of her rolled *yoh* in the corner of the entryway as the first weak rays of light broke through the black, predawn sky. Then she walked into the kitchen to retrieve the wicker basket she had filled with foods they could eat on the road. In order to avoid the need to wash breakfast dishes, she had fixed a light meal of hard-boiled eggs and apple slices, and she added these items to the foodstuffs that she and *Sahmonim* had prepared the day before.

After she deposited the basket next to her mounting pile of travel necessities, she moved from window to window throughout the living room and kitchen, first lowering, then latching the shutters in preparation to leave.

She had yet to see anyone stirring about the cabin, but the upstairs floorboards creaked under heavy footsteps and, earlier, the shower had been running for a good long while, so she surmised that Jennifer was also awake and getting ready.

Eun-Me wondered if everyone else had slept as fitfully as she had during the night. She had tossed and turned, with her ears tuned to listen for a warning clang of the chapel bell. Yet, when her alarm clock sounded to signal a new day, she had breathed a prayer of thanksgiving that the night hours had been calm.

A knock sounded at the cabin's front door at the same moment that the three members of the Woods family came down the stairs toting their suitcases behind them. "I'll get that," Eun-Me said, skirting around them to answer the door as they fumbled to don their shoes.

Moksanim and *Sahmonim* Carroll stood in the shadows of the porch stoop. They each held a lethargic boy. A tall duffel bag drooped between them. Eun-Me flung the door open wide and invited them inside.

"We won't bother coming in," *Moksanim* Carroll said, patting his son's back. "The Taylors and Professor Spencer are coming right behind us. But if we could get the keys to the car, we could lay our boys in the backseat while we load the vehicles."

Philip jangled a key ring above his head. "Follow me. I'm ready now." He scooped up Eun-Me's *yoh* and tucked it under his arm as he headed out the door.

"I'll be back for the rest of this stuff in just a minute. Mom, can you rouse Jennifer and tell her to get her suitcase out here? I'm sure hers is the biggest piece of luggage we'll have to deal with, and we need to pack it first."

"Here I come. Just hold your horses." Jennifer skulked out of her bedroom, pushing her suitcase ahead of her in swift shoves. "Actually, I could use your help." She straightened and arched her shoulders back.

Moksanim Woods left his own baggage by the stairs in order to assist her, and she followed him outside. Eun-Me hoisted her pack across her back and held the door open for *Sahmonim*. Together, they joined the others by the vehicles. The Carrolls were situating their boys in the back of the car while everyone else watched Philip and his father wrestle to lift Jennifer's suitcase into the trunk of the car.

"I don't know what kind of seating arrangements you had in mind, but I'd be grateful if our family could stay together," *Sahmonim* Carroll said as she approached the group. "I'm so frantic with worry that I can't bear the thought of being separated from my husband right now. Besides, I need his help with the boys."

Philip wiped the dust from his hands as he straightened. "We haven't really considered who will sit where, other than the drivers' seats. I'll be driving the truck and Dad will be behind the wheel of the car."

"I call dibs on the car, too," Jennifer interjected. Eun-Me caught Philip rolling his eyes at this latest demand.

Eun-Me kept silent in the ensuing shuffle for seats while *Moksanim* and *Sahmonim* Carroll each scooped a child in their lap and then eased into the backseat of the car. After the stout, gray-haired *Sahmonim* Taylor wedged in beside the young mother, Philip's father returned his seat back to its upright position and took his place behind the wheel. *Sahmonim* Woods straddled the gearshift next to her husband, and Jennifer hopped in beside her to occupy the seat next to the window. The car door slammed shut with a thud, leaving Eun-Me standing in the drive.

She didn't feel as though she had any right to demand a certain place or position. However, she squirmed uncomfortably when she found herself seated between Philip and the tall and lanky Professor Spencer, with *Moksanim* Taylor sitting next to the passenger door. She would have offered to ride in the open back rather than the close confines of the cab, but the men had loaded the truck bed with gas cans and hurriedly gathered tarps and camping supplies.

"I hope you won't be too miserable riding with us guys, but we're running short on open seats." Philip reached around the wheel to the steering column and turned the key in the ignition. He looked at Eun-Me with a sympathetic smile while the engine chortled into action. "Besides, I need to be able to reach the gearshift, and you're by far the most petite one among us, so you're elected to sit by me."

His hand brushed her knee as he took hold of the stick shift and ground the gears from neutral into first, then eased his foot off the clutch, lunging the vehicle forward. The casual sweep of his hand across her leg sent an electrifying shiver through her.

Philip extended his arm to adjust the rearview mirror, and Eun-Me lifted her gaze to catch him looking at her. She could only see the reflection of his eyes, but she knew from his crinkled squint that he was smiling at her. The brief magnetic interchange that ensued brought an instant heat to her cheeks, and she had to willfully avert her eyes.

Acting rather discombobulated at the tender moment, Philip cleared his throat and twisted his head to look out the back window. "Looks like Dad's right behind us. I guess we're off."

Eun-Me scoffed at herself for reading more into Philip's actions than he meant to convey. She hastened to convince herself that he was trying to put her at ease. Nothing more. She would never be, *must* never be, anything other than an old family friend turned *ajumoni*. For that privilege alone, she felt unending gratitude. Yet she would harbor this fresh memory of Philip's comfort and concern long after he was gone.

He steered the truck through the compound gate, leading their small procession due east down the rutted road of soggy earth. The route that Philip and his father had mapped out the day before avoided the main roads in hopes of dodging any troop movements. As the crow flies, *Moksanim*

Woods had said, the distance between Taechon Beach and the city of Daejon spanned roughly sixty miles. But he anticipated that the journey would take them eight or nine hours, or more, as they traversed the back roads around and through the mountainous countryside.

Eun-Me stared at her folded hands in silence while the three men carried the conversation. When they switched topics from the encroaching enemy armies and the pros-pects of war to Korean and American politics, she didn't even try to follow their discussion, for they used too many English vocabulary words that were unfamiliar to her. But *Moksanim* Taylor's words jarred her from her daydreams when he leaned around the professor to address Philip.

"So, tell me, Son. What is the story behind the pretty young blond riding back there with your folks?" The elder missionary ran a hand over his bald head. "She blew my theory that she was your future missus when she chose to ride with your parents rather than next to you. Is she a new missionary recruit?" He elbowed the bachelor profes-sor in the arm and chuckled. "There may be hope for you after all, Spencer."

Without turning her head, Eun-Me cast a sideways glance at Philip, and her stomach knotted to see the bloodless pallor that had settled over his face.

A quick snort preceded Philip's response.

"I think I can predict with certainty that Miss Anderson is not the answer to our good professor's prayers for a wife. Let it suffice to say that she is my boss's daughter and she came to Korea on a fact-finding mission. Thanks to this Communist invasion, I'm now faced with the unpleasant responsibility of seeing her transported safely back to San Francisco."

A sudden and sad realization gripped Eun-Me as she considered for the first time that Philip might accompany Miss Jennifer back to the States. For some reason, she had assumed that he would find her an escort or send her on alone while he stayed the remainder of the summer with his parents, as planned. She wasn't ready to say good-bye to Philip yet. He'd only arrived days before. They had so much catching up to do, and she had waited so long.

Up until his arrival last Friday, she had almost convinced herself that what she felt for Philip was nothing more than the remnants of a teenager's affection. She'd heard the Americans describe these feelings as a "crush" or "puppy love."

After all, she'd been brought up to believe that romantic love was just another cockamamie American idea. In Korea, love came long after the wedding day—if it ever came—after years of growing comfortable with the mate chosen by one's parents.

Eun-Me stole a flickering glimpse at Philip. The jumble of emotions she felt for him caused her to question everything she had been taught about love. Despite their lengthy separation, her affections for Philip had blossomed rather than withered from the neglect of years and miles. She could neither explain nor understand this connection between them. Often, through a simple exchanged glance, they read the other's thoughts. Without saying a word, they were able to acknowledge that the other knew.

The longer he stayed, the deeper the connection grew. Just being with him made her happy. He filled the empty spaces of her soul.

She allowed a secret smile to play on her lips at the thought of how special he made her feel. He never treated her as a lowly servant or acted condescending toward her. He treated her like she was special. Like a lady. A queen.

What she felt for him went far beyond comfort, and sometimes felt far from comfortable. Sometimes the sight of him set her heart racing in a way she'd never experienced before, and she knew she'd never experience with another. This had to be love. However, such feelings held no future promise of fulfillment. He could never know the extent of her affections. Philip would go back to America and find a new bride or patch things up with Jennifer. And when he went, he would take a piece of her heart with him.

She consoled herself with the thought that, perhaps, God in His mercy knew her heart couldn't withstand the humiliation she would encounter if Philip were to learn of her true feelings for him. Her affections were getting harder and harder to hide. His speedy departure might be a blessing in disguise.

Eun-Me jumped when the deep bellow of a car horn sliced the air and, in syncopation with her fellow travelers, she turned her head to look back at the Studebaker. The car slowed to a crawl and pulled to the side of the road, but had not yet come to a complete stop when the passenger door flew open and Miss Jennifer jumped out.

❦

Philip pumped the brakes and brought the lumbering truck to a halt. Then, shifting into reverse, he twisted around and slid his right arm across the seat back behind Eun-Me so that he could see out the back window. Within seconds, he closed the distance between the two vehicles and parked the truck in the middle of the road.

He jumped from the cab and ran back to the car. His mother had already climbed out, waving for Philip to catch up to her as she made her way toward Jennifer.

"She's been really quiet since we left the cabin. Then, all of a sudden, she said to stop the car. That she was going to be sick."

Philip and his mother came up behind Jennifer, who had fallen to her knees on the edge of a barley field and was heaving up her stomach's contents.

"Mom, she's going to need a drink of water and a wet cloth when she's done. Would you mind asking Grace to dig those things up while I stay here and watch over Jennifer?"

His mother nodded her assent and began to walk back toward the road.

Philip knelt on one knee at Jennifer's side and pulled her hair away from her face. When her retching stopped, she leaned back and hugged her knees to her chest.

"I feel like I'm coming right out of my skin," she said, resting her head on her knees.

"I worried that something like this might happen. You're going through the worst of the withdrawal symptoms as you flush those sedatives out of your system." He started to pat her on the back, but she shrugged his hand away. "I'm really sorry for you, Jennifer. I wish there was something I could do to help, but you should start feeling better soon."

"You could help me if you really wanted to." She lifted her face to reveal tears spilling down both cheeks. They dripped from her chin, leaving dark wet splotches on her red pedal pushers.

"I'll fetch the milk of magnesia from my bag to help settle your stomach, but if you're asking me to give you another sedative—I just can't do that." He shook his head emphatically.

"Please, Philip. Won't you take into consideration these extenuating circumstances? I'll never survive this grueling car trip. We're bouncing all over the road." Suddenly, her head dropped down and she covered her face with her hand. "Oh, I feel faint," she mumbled.

As Philip took her in his arms to keep her from lying in the soft, black dirt, he felt an overwhelming sympathy for her. Real compassion. Pity for the poor little rich girl. But nothing more. The feelings of love he had held for her until very recently had been replaced with a cumbersome sense of duty to deliver Jennifer, safe and sound, back to her daddy. A silent prayer of gratitude flowed through his thoughts when he considered that this discovery came before he had married her.

He looked up to see Grace and his mother approaching, and his heart pounded in his chest at the sight of his dear old friend.

Philip shook his head, wondering if he was going crazy. He'd known Grace practically his whole life. He'd never viewed her as anything other than a real buddy and pal. He struggled to think of a reasonable explanation for his emotional reaction to watching her approach. He certainly could not begin to entertain any romantic notions. Especially now. Probably never.

There were far too many reasons why a relationship with Grace would never work. For one thing, he still had a residency program to complete in the States. And if he'd learned anything from his breakup with Jennifer, he learned that he shouldn't expect any woman to pick up roots and follow him halfway around the world.

Grace would be as miserable in America as Jennifer was in Korea.

He rose and hovered over the women as they assumed their nursing duties. With the utmost care, Grace tended to Jennifer's needs. She eased her head forward and offered a sip of water, then mopped her forehead with a damp hand towel. She was born to be a mother. She needed a husband and children to pamper and coddle. How unfair that this culture's traditions would deprive her of the privilege because she had no family to strike a marriage deal and pay a dowry.

Maybe, just maybe, he could pursue these romantic feelings when he returned as a missionary doctor after his residency. However, until then, he could not allow himself to even dwell on such things. In the meantime, the Lord might mercifully and miraculously bring some Korean man into her life who would accept Grace for his wife despite her orphan status.

For now, he needed to purge himself of any thoughts about women and romance and concentrate on the problems at hand. He had to get Jennifer back in the car and all of them back on the road. They hadn't received any updated reports on the invasion since yesterday. Neither his transistor nor the car radio could pick up anything but static. And he had no idea whether or not their forces were successful in pushing the Communist troops out of Seoul. Everyone in their little convoy would be on edge until they were able to get to Daejon and hear the latest news.

He crouched next to Grace and studied Jennifer's face. "How's the ailing passenger?"

Ignoring his question, Jennifer waved off Grace. "I just shouldn't have tried to eat anything in the car." She pointed her comments to his mother as she accepted her assistance to stand, then looped an arm through her crooked elbow.

Either she had decided the effort to push him for another sedative was useless, or she didn't want his mother and Grace to know the true reason behind her sudden illness. Whatever her rationale for dropping her appeal, he was grateful for the unspoken truce.

"Well, I'll race to the truck and dig out that milk of magnesia. You just take your time and let Mom and Grace help you." When he came over the rise at the roadside, he found all the other passengers milling about and stretching their legs. His dad and Professor Spencer had spread a road map across the hood of the car and were deep in discussion about possible detour routes should the need arise.

Philip pulled back the tarp on the truck bed and was opening his bag on the tailgate to retrieve the medicine for Jennifer when he felt someone tugging on his pant leg.

"Hey, Mr. Doctor," Caleb, the younger Carroll boy, called out, "why'd that pretty lady urp over there?" Instantly, his mother clapped a hand over his mouth.

"Don't mind him. He's not yet mastered the art of tact." Mrs. Carroll allowed her hand to drop to her son's collar as she spoke, but she still maintained firm control over him. "I explained that some people get a little queasy when riding in a car, but I guess he wants a second opinion."

The youngster looked up with brown eyes as round as silver dollars, and Philip stooped to ruffle the boy's auburn hair. "Your momma is right, Caleb. Miss Anderson's tummy is just a little upset from the bouncing and jostling, is all. She'll be fine. But you could help her feel better if you'd sit still and quiet in the car. Do you think you could do that for me?"

His little head wobbled up and down in exaggerated assent. "Know what? I got to water the trees. And my dad's takin' Michael—"

"Caleb!" Mrs. Carroll's hand smothered her son's mouth once more in an effort to silence him, but he still managed to mumble the remainder of his announcement.

"—to water a tree, too."

Philip tipped back his head and laughed. "Actually, Mrs. Carroll, I was just about to suggest that we all ought to do the same before we get back on the road."

The women had not yet come into view, so he deduced that they must have stopped at a discreet clump of bushes at the edge of the barley field for just such a purpose. Across the road and a short distance away, he saw Michael and his father stepping from behind a piney knoll.

Once everyone's needs were tended to and Philip had administered a dose of the chalk-white medicine to Jennifer, they resumed their earlier positions and the caravan started off again.

At every chuck hole they confronted for the next several miles, Philip would snatch a quick glance in the rearview mirror to check on Jennifer's reaction and make certain that the Studebaker hadn't pulled over again. But she maintained a granite expression and a statuesque pose. No one in the truck seemed to want to bother with conversation, each one withdrawing into their own private thoughts as the truck creaked and groaned over the bumpy road.

They stopped on the outskirts of a rural village for lunch, refueling, and a "tree-watering" break, but the skies were heavy with rain and not even the little boys dawdled over their meal.

The further inland they drove, the more dramatically the scenery changed. The flat fields of barley gave way to terraced rice paddies, ripened to a verdant green, cut into rolling hills. Philip had expected to encounter scores of fleeing refugees. Instead, they saw only farmers standing behind an oxen-driven plow, goading their beasts forward through the mud. The only uniforms they sighted were those of the occasional stooped-shouldered *haraboji* as they strolled alongside the road. Each old gentleman wore an identical long white robe, with the outline of a topknot visible through his opaque horsehair hat. They all shuffled as though their feet were heavy, their eyes scanning the distant hills.

With even less frequency, they would drive past a *halmoni*, dressed in traditional ballooning skirts of bleached muslin, a baby tied up in a blanket on her back.

"These folks seem oblivious to the events going on in Seoul," Philip said to no one in particular. Inwardly, he cringed to think that they might go barreling into Daejon like a bunch of wild-eyed refugees only to discover that the crisis had been squelched no sooner than it had begun. Even so, he concluded that he would rather be a safe dolt than a dead hero.

"News travels slow out here, so they may very well not know," Grace whispered. "But more likely, even if they have heard, people out in the countryside would refuse to leave their land unless the enemy is in sight."

"Let's pray that none of us faces such a time," Professor Spencer interjected as a final amen, and they fell silent again.

When the terrain shifted from rolling hills to steep mountains, driving required all of Philip's attentions, and he was thankful for the lull in conversation. He squinted in such intense concentration whenever they crept around the precipitous hairpin curves that his temples throbbed. The dirt road frequently dwindled to nothing more than an ox path, and the clutches of both vehicles began to emit an acrid smell from the constant downshifting.

The repeated blare of the Studebaker's horn broke Philip's concentration as they chugged up the side of a mountain. He looked into the rearview mirror in time to see the car disappear around a curve, rolling backward down the dirt lane they had just traveled.

six

"What's the matter? Are they okay?" Grace shifted in the seat next to him and craned her neck to see out the rear window.

"My guess is, he's burned out his clutch," Reverend Taylor answered for Philip while he maneuvered the truck to a stop. "Pray his brakes hold."

Philip cut the engine and his door squeaked open while he scrambled out of the cab. "I don't like the idea of driving this monster in reverse. Everybody stay here while I run and find out what the problem is. Hopefully, Dad was able to stop just around the bend." He left the door ajar and followed the fresh tire tracks down the hill in the direction the car had just gone.

Gravel skittered down the hill ahead of him, forcing him to shuffle to keep from losing his footing. His dad had managed to pull the car into a scenic turnout and was lifting the hood when he approached. Even though Philip had asked everyone to wait in the truck, the other men caught up to him, and they all gathered around to gape at the steaming engine while Grace joined the women and children clustered behind them.

"This buggy won't be going on to Daejon today." Philip's dad whacked the fender with his fist. "And who knows where or when we'll ever find a replacement clutch in these parts. God bless the women of the Texas Diocese

94

Missionary Society, but when they gifted us with this automobile, I don't think they considered the difficulty of finding parts for a Studebaker on a mission field."

"Whatever will we do, Clarence?" asked Philip's mother as she squeezed in beside his dad and circled his forearm between her hands.

"We've only got one option that I can see." Scratching his head, he turned away from the car and looked up the road. "Somehow, we'll all have to pile into the back of the truck."

"You can't be serious!" Jennifer growled, crossing her arms. "I'm barely able to manage the car ride. You might as well shoot me here and now rather than force me to endure even an hour in the back of that junk heap."

Tempted to take her up on her offer, Philip let loose with a snide retort. "You're free to walk the rest of the way if you'd rather—"

"Don't you think she could ride up front?" Grace's voice drifted out from behind the others and interrupted him, deflating his escalating anger.

"I'll be glad to give her my seat. She is sick, after all."

Sweet, gracious Grace displayed more Christian charity than he could ever possess. He didn't want her to give up her place next to him. His right side still radiated from the closeness of Grace after riding side by side for the past several hours.

He treasured the memory of her nearness.

Even if he hadn't stated his feelings for her in words, he knew she understood how he felt. For, despite his resolve not to become any more emotionally involved with Grace than he already was, they had traded countless quick glances and silent exchanges in the rearview mirror throughout the course of the day.

He felt certain Grace shared his growing affection. She conveyed as much each time she caught him looking at her. He cringed to think that Jennifer might be riding beside him for the duration of their trip to Daejon. After their breakup, the thought of sitting next to her for even a minute or two sent ice water through his veins.

Philip looked from Grace to Jennifer and back again as he tried to think of some way to accommodate Jennifer without making himself miserable.

"Son, you look like you could use a break." While he spoke, his dad wiped the grease off his hands with a faded red rag he had pulled from under the driver's seat. "If you don't mind riding in the back, I'll drive the truck."

Philip made a mental note to thank him for his merciful intervention at the first chance he got.

Mrs. Taylor waved her hand to summon his dad's attention. "What do you propose we do with all our baggage? We couldn't possibly squeeze into that truck with all our suitcases, too."

"I think we should take our example from Grace and gather a small bundle of one change of clothes and basic toiletries." While he spoke, Philip's dad twisted his rag in his hands and kicked at the dirt, sending a small stone tumbling over the side of the precipice. "We'll pack as much as we can in the car with the hope that we will be able to return within the next twenty-four hours to repair the clutch and retrieve our—"

The other missionaries nodded their assent, but Jennifer launched a vehement protest before he could finish his proposal. "That's fine for all you folks who live around here, but I'm on my way back to the States. Couldn't we enlist one of these little guys to sit on top of my luggage?" She ticked her head toward the Carroll boys, who each clutched the legs of a parent. "That wouldn't take up too much space. Or couldn't you tie my suitcase onto the roof? I asked earlier for someone to bring a rope for me. Did anyone do that?"

Philip grimaced at the thought of having to lift Jennifer's suitcase onto the top of the truck. Even if they were able to get the thing up there, the weight might cave in the roof. With a lot less effort, she could take her daddy's money and replace her fancy clothes. Besides, those now-useless bridal catalogues accounted for most of the bag's weight. When her time came to marry someone more in keeping with the lifestyle she sought, she could and would buy a brand new set of catalogues and magazines.

He kneaded the inside of his bottom lip between his teeth in an attempt to bite back a bitter retort, but his dad interceded for him once again when he turned toward Jennifer, his expression shifting to a frown. "I understand your predicament, but we're in a crisis situation here, Miss Anderson, and any extra space we can eke out around the passengers must be filled with essentials, not your wardrobe. We'll be straining the truck's transmission enough trying to carry twelve passengers up and down these mountain roads, and we'd have a mighty long walk to Daejon if that vehicle breaks down, too. You'll need to follow the same restrictions that we're imposing on everyone else."

"Fine, then." She glared at Philip through slitted eyes.

"Can I trouble you to unload my bag so I can pull out my necessities?"

As he spun away from her and walked toward the trunk of the car, she muttered loud enough for all to hear, "I might as well kiss the rest of my belongings good-bye."

❦

Eun-Me gave her head a quick jerk to dispel the mental picture sparked by Miss Jennifer's remark. She believed that the act of kissing ought to be reserved for someone much more precious than possessions.

Even though she had never kissed nor been kissed by any man, she often fantasized about the prospect of her first kiss. Philip's kiss. The mere words made her mouth tingle with the sweet, tangible illusion of his lips pressing tenderly against hers.

She forced herself to tuck away her intimate reveries and return to the real world. Such daydreams could never be fulfilled. With Philip or any man. She reached out from her position behind the others and tapped Miss Jennifer on the elbow. "I could help you, if you'd like. I don't have any repacking to do."

"I believe I'll take you up on your offer." Miss Jennifer pressed her fingertips into her temple and closed her eyes. "I have such a pounding headache. I don't think I could bend over right now." She dropped her hand to her side and turned to follow after Philip while Eun-Me fell into step behind her.

As Eun-Me culled through the stacks of carefully folded clothes in search of something practical, Miss Jennifer towered over her, tapping at her mouth with a red-polished fingernail. "Uh-uh," she grunted each time that Eun-Me's hand lingered on an article of clothing she thought might be appropriate.

The only undergarments she found were lighter-than-air scraps of lace-trimmed silk. By comparison, her own cotton pantaloons seemed so. . .well, *utilitarian*. No wonder the American seemed to glide when she walked while Eun-Me crinkled and plodded along. She'd never seen such delicate apparel among Mrs. Woods's laundry. She decided that only the richest of "big noses" could afford these flimsy, fancy fineries. A small sigh escaped her lips when she patted three pairs of the panties into the bottom of the straw beach bag Miss Jennifer had given her to pack.

By the time Eun-Me had gleaned two complete outfits and essential toiletries from Miss Jennifer's suitcase, the others had finished shuttling all but the most crucial supplies from the back of the truck and into the car. Philip stood at the truck's open tailgate and motioned for her to hand him the overstuffed beach bag.

"Here, Dad." He tossed the parcel up to his father, who was rimming the truck bed with everyone's knapsacks. "This should be the last."

Turning back to Eun-Me, Philip's eyebrows raised in question as he spoke. "I hope you don't mind. We took the liberty of spreading your *yoh* out flat to give our backsides a little extra padding."

"No, of course not. Whatever I can do to help." She noted that they had lined the rusty sheet metal floor with a canvas tarp before laying down her bedroll. "Is there anything else I can carry back to the car?"

"Naw. You've done more than your share just by assisting Jennifer." He sent a quick wink her way, and the innocent gesture made Eun-Me's pulse race. "Dad estimates that we're no more than an hour and a half away from Daejon. We should pull into the city about dusk—if we don't run into any more trouble, that is. I think we're all ready for a rest stop and a hot meal."

Only an hour and a half away. And then what? Eun-Me wrestled with the possibilities. If the invading Communists continued to push south across the peninsula, not only would Philip flee Korea with Jennifer, but his parents might accompany them as well.

Then she'd be left utterly, totally alone.

Yet, even as the thought slashed into her mind, her father's favorite and oft-repeated scriptural promise brought comfort to her soul. *"Be strong and of good courage, fear not, nor be afraid of them: for the LORD thy God, he it is that doth go with thee; he will not fail thee, nor forsake thee."* She closed her eyes and inhaled deeply, drawing strength from the knowledge that her Lord would not forsake her, no matter what the future held.

When *Moksanim* Woods bellowed, "All aboard," everyone but Eun-Me and Philip began jockeying for position. *Sahmonim* Woods sat beside her husband in the truck cab and *Sahmonim* Taylor squeezed in next to her. Miss Jennifer, whining that she might need to make another emergency exit, occupied the seat by the door.

Philip stayed back to offer a steadying hand while the remaining passengers climbed into the truck bed, and Eun-Me hoped that she appeared humble and deferring as she waited off to one side. She would have let the others go first anyway, but this time she had an ulterior motive for lagging behind. If she managed things just right, she would be sitting next to Philip for the remainder of the ride.

She watched *Moksanim* Taylor crawl into the center of the truck and lean his head back against the rear window of the cab. Next, the Carroll family spread out across the left side of the flatbed so that Michael and Caleb would have room enough to wiggle away their nervous energy. Finally, Professor Spencer hoisted himself into the truck bed and nestled among the knapsacks in the corner directly behind Miss Jennifer.

"Madam. Your carriage awaits." Philip held one arm across his waist and bowed low while cutting a wide swath through the air with his outstretched hand. She accepted his assistance, but knew if she looked in his eyes, she wouldn't be able to maintain an appropriate expression of solemnity, so she glanced forward instead, just in time to catch a look of disgust from Miss Jennifer.

The split-second interchange left Eun-Me feeling like a fool. She scrambled to make room for Philip, and while he yanked the tailgate shut behind him, she drew her knees up under her chin.

Sometime during their repacking efforts, the sun had evaporated the rain clouds. Oppressive midday heat soaked the moisture from the steaming earth like a poultice, and a fog of exhaust billowed around the truck when the engine rumbled to a start. Once they were under way, a dust cloud enveloped them, forcing Eun-Me to bury her face in her hands.

At first, she was grateful for the opportunity to recover from her embarrassment without the risk of Philip wondering why she had withdrawn so suddenly. But the more she thought about Miss Jennifer, the more she resolved to hold her head up high. She wasn't about to let that sophisticated crank rob her of these snatches of joy she found in Philip's company.

Every few minutes, she tried to lift her head and take in her surroundings. She wanted another opportunity to look Miss Jennifer straight in the eye and smile ever so sweetly. But each time the irritating haze clogged her throat and made her eyes fill with cleansing tears.

Catching quick glimpses at her traveling companions, she saw that they had all chosen to sleep rather than fight to see through the gritty haze. She refused to succumb to the tug of drowsiness. She wanted to cherish each moment she had left with Philip until he departed for America. The memories she gathered now might have to last her another several years. Or forever.

Eun-Me marveled at Philip's ability to sleep, for he looked terribly uncomfortable. He had tucked his knees up under his chin and laced his fingers together across the back of his head. But his relaxed body bobbed and swayed with the rocking motion of the truck. Each time a tire bounced into a pothole or over a rock, his form leaned into her leg, sending goose bumps prickling up her left side. The farther down the road they traveled, it seemed to Eun-Me that the jostling encounters with Philip occurred with greater frequency. She pondered the possibility that Philip was intentionally knocking into her. However, she decided that, with her eyes closed, her senses were merely heightened and her imagination had gone wild.

The next time his weight pressed into her knee, she noted with surprise that they hadn't hit any bumps in the road. She spread her fingers apart from her covered eyes and stole a peek at him. Poking his head out from under his arm, his eyes sparkled with mischief as the distinguished doctor twisted his features into a funny face and stuck out his tongue at her.

Eun-Me quickly closed the gap between her fingers, and her palms felt the heat rising in her cheeks. When they were kids, Philip had always played such childish pranks on her when attempting to take her mind off a tense situation. Yet, even though she knew all this, she couldn't control the flush of pleasure flooding over her—until the unwelcome memory of Miss Jennifer's earlier sneer attacked her thoughts.

Despite her resolve to do otherwise, Eun-Me berated her giddy reaction to Philip's teasing and forced herself to regain a modicum of dignity.

With a final bone-jarring jolt, the truck bounced off of the dirt path and up onto a stretch of paved road. Philip jabbed Eun-Me lightly with his elbow and leaned toward her to whisper in her ear. "You are probably safe to put your hands down. Looks like we won't have to eat any more dust for awhile. We should be pulling into town soon."

Lifting her face out of her hands, Eun-Me could see Philip stretching his arms above his head and working the stiffness out of his limbs. Rather than the occasional thatch-roofed farmhouse rising up from the rice paddy landscape, now black-tiled rooftops surrounded by whitewashed courtyards sprouted like mushrooms along the pedestrian-clogged street.

"This paved road adds a whole new meaning to the saying, 'A sight for sore eyes.' I don't think I could have endured another pothole."

A sight for sore eyes. Eun-Me committed the new English phrase to memory as Philip reached for his back pocket and pulled out a clean, folded hanky, then handed it discreetly to her. "You look like you've had about all the traveling adventures you could stand for one day, too."

She grimaced to think what she must look like and accepted the handkerchief with a silently mouthed, "Thank you." She'd heard some of the other *ajumonis* say that the Americans they worked for used a handkerchief to blow their nose, and then would actually return the soiled article to their pockets. Eun-Me knew Philip would never do anything so uncouth. After a couple of swipes over her face, she tucked the dust-coated cloth up into her sleeve. Provided they stopped in Daejon long enough for things to dry, she intended to rinse it out once they reached the military compound. She ached in places she'd never even noticed before and wondered if she would be wrong to pray for a good hot bath.

A child's shrill wail drew her focus back to the truck. "Momma, Michael's lookin' at me." Caleb Carroll poked at his mother with a pudgy finger to punctuate his whine. "Make him stop."

The weariness expressed in his mother's response reflected Eun-Me's own utter exhaustion.

❦

When his father pulled to the side of the road a second time to study Lieutenant Barnard's hand-scribbled directions to the KMAG compound, Philip wondered if they had made a wrong turn. He worried even more when, instead of taking the highway toward downtown Daejon, they headed northwest onto a hard-packed gravel road leading into a small village. He was ready to crawl up to the window behind the driver's seat and ask if he could help when they fell into line behind a camouflaged U.S. military jeep. Both vehicles ground to a stop in front of a barricade at the end of the isolated road.

The few remaining splinters of daylight illuminated an American MP as he stepped from a small guardhouse. He raised the barricade and waved the jeep through, but blocked their path by standing directly in front of their vehicle with his rifle gripped in both hands and ready to use.

"Halt. Who goes there?"

Philip leapfrogged over the truck's tailgate and joined his dad beside the truck while the MP approached. The closer he got, the less intimidating the soldier became. Philip thought the young buck private looked more like a kid dressed up to play army in his father's old fatigues than a modern-day warrior trained to kill the enemy.

In the fading light, Philip could make out several wooden structures and a number of Quonset huts situated on the compound in neat rows. Gusting winds unfurled the Stars and Stripes atop a flagpole that towered just beyond the guardhouse, and the flag's hooks and grommets clanked loudly against the metal mast.

"We are a group of American missionaries and our dependents." Philip's father looked the soldier in the eye without flinching. "We were sent here by an officer with the Far East Command's Korean Liaison Office. He said you'd be able to advise us as to the current military crisis and provide us with food, shelter, and an escort to safe haven, if necessary."

"I'll need to see passports and proper identification

before I can admit you onto the compound. We're under tight security." The GI tilted his head to look past Philip and survey the truck's passengers. Philip could tell when his gaze reached Jennifer, for his eyebrows raised and a fleeting smirk of lecherous admiration crossed his face.

Philip developed an instant dislike for the private, and his blood boiled to see pond scum like this kid looking at Jennifer—or any woman—with such blatant lust. The fact that the guy was serving his country far away from home still didn't give him license to be disrespectful. Regardless of Philip's personal feelings about Jennifer, he wouldn't hesitate to defend her honor.

The soldier made brief eye contact with him and grinned, confirming Philip's interpretation of the man's expression, then he continued to scan the rest of the truck's passengers. Philip knew the moment the GI noticed Grace, huddled by the rear wheel well.

The soldier's smirk dropped into a frown. His entire face hardened. He cleared his throat. "I can't let the civilian *gook* pass. We have no way of telling which ones are the enemy and which aren't. Like I told you, we're under tight security, and I'm only supposed to let verifiable Americans in until Major Denton tells me otherwise."

Seething even more at the private's use of the racial slur aimed at Grace, Philip couldn't keep the sarcasm from his response. "I'm sure you meant no discourtesy to our Miss Cho, but the proper term for a Korean in their language is *'Hangook saram,'* and to my knowledge, there is no abbreviation. How would you like it if I were to call you a —"

"Son, this isn't the time or place for a language lesson." His father laid a hand on Philip's shoulder. "Why don't you collect everyone's passports and Grace's registration card while I arrange to discuss this matter with the private's commanding officer?"

He started to walk away to gather the documents, but his step faltered when he heard his dad address the young MP. "Before I joined the Lord's Army, I served as a master sergeant in the U.S. Army myself, so I understand the chain of command and your need to follow orders. . . ."

Philip looked back in time to see the private stiffen at his dad's subtle rank-pulling pronouncement. He continued on his way, grimacing to think of the trouble that he'd be in about now if not for his father's levelheaded intervention. He had allowed his quick temper to get the best of him again—even though he knew full well that a gentle reply like his dad's, which related to the annoying soldier's predicament, might have garnered a more accommodating response.

As Philip returned from assembling the requested bundle of documents, he rubbed his thumb over the black-and-white, solemn-faced photo of Grace attached to her registration card.

"Oh, Lord," he prayed with his eyes open while he walked, "protect Your precious Grace from further tragedy."

He deposited the official papers into the MP's outstretched hand and watched while the soldier turned on his heels and reentered his guardhouse. After thumbing through their credentials, he began to mumble something into a walkie-talkie. But, no matter how hard Philip strained to hear the GI's monologue, his words were still unintelligible.

His dad tugged on his sleeve to draw him toward the front of the truck and out of the MP's line of vision.

"When I go to meet with the major and discuss our situation, why don't you pull the truck over and encourage everyone to get out and stretch their legs? The troops are getting rather restless, and Michael and Caleb appear to have declared war on one another."

High-pitched squeals split the early evening air.

"At times like this, I'm reminded why we only wanted one child. Whenever you fought with Eun-Soo or Grace, we could just shoo them off to their *omma*." His father shot a quick glance over his shoulder toward Grace. "I hope Grace didn't catch wind that she's the reason for our delay. She'd feel terrible if she knew."

"And I hope I didn't compound our problem by spouting off to the MP." Philip snatched a sideways glimpse at the guardhouse, and when he did, his father whispered into his good ear.

"If God and your mother hadn't been watching, I might have decked the bum. Might still if he doesn't wipe that seedy grin off his face whenever he looks at Jennifer. Don't worry, though. He's low man on the totem pole at this dinky outpost. Let's just pray that his commanding officer is a man of reason and integrity."

"Excuse me, Sir." The MP slung his rifle over his shoulder as he approached. "Don't mean to interrupt, but Major Denton has agreed to speak with you immediately. He's ordering the mess sergeant to rustle up some grub for your group, and they can go on to the mess hall while you meet with the major." Philip hiked his eyebrows in suspicion at the soldier's about-face in attitude.

"I'm not allowed to leave my post, and we're short-handed, since most of our men have already been called out, so you'll have to go unescorted, but both buildings are easy enough to find. The large Quonset hut in the center over there is the mess hall." He held their documents in his hand, so he pointed with a nod of his head toward the half-moon-shaped corrugated metal building as he spoke. "Located just north of that you'll find the major. There. Where the jeep is parked. If you have any trouble, just look at the signs." The soldier handed the thick pile of passports back to Philip's father, then snapped his right hand away from his forehead in salute. "You're all free to pass."

"Including Miss Cho?" Philip hesitated to ask, but they had to know.

"Yes. Including Miss Cho."

❦

Eun-Me eased down from the tailgate with Philip's aid, and then she leaned against the spindly trunk of a gingko tree while he helped the others disembark. She knew she ought to follow custom and rush ahead to hold the door for her superiors, but the unfamiliar surroundings left her frozen in fear and nervousness.

She felt more and more out of place among all these foreigners. She had caught the angry expression on the guard's face when he first noticed her among the missionaries. And, although she couldn't hear his words, his eyes had shouted that she wasn't welcome here.

"Are you feeling a bit uncertain about eating dinner in a place called a 'mess hall'?" *Sahmonim* Woods came alongside her and patted her lightly on the forearm. "You'll see. It's not as bad as it sounds. Come on. Walk with me."

She must have noticed Eun-Me's searching gaze for Philip, because *Sahmonim* answered her question before she could ask. "Clarence had asked to speak with the man in charge and Philip went along. I'm sure they'll bring us an update concerning the invasion, but there's no sense in us waiting for them. I'm so hungry I could eat a team of oxen about now." She had to raise her voice to be heard over the ruckus the Carroll brothers were creating as they ran past them toward the entrance, arguing over which one should get to enter first. Their father settled the squabble by serving as the doorkeeper himself, and he made both boys wait next to him.

"Excuse me. You'll have to excuse me." Miss Jennifer shuffled and danced her way to the front of the group and through the open door. "I've got to find the little girl's room. Quick!" The others ignored her dramatics and filed in behind her.

A blast of bright light and loud music engulfed them when Eun-Me and *Sahmonim* stepped across the threshold and into the wide hall filled with tables and chairs.

"Welcome to our little piece of America right here in *kimchee* land." A short and round man dressed all in white stepped from behind a work area surrounded by a serving counter in the back of the room. As he approached, he wiped his hands on his apron, which left an oily brown smear across the hem. "My orders are to make you feel right at home, and I've already thrown a couple dozen hamburger patties on my grill. I'll keep 'em comin' until you've had your fill. You folks go ahead and make your-selves comfortable." He headed back behind the counter and picked up a greasy spatula. "Burgers 'n' fries will be comin' right up. If you need anything in the meantime, just holler, 'Sarge.' "

He began to flip the sizzling meat and while he worked, he sang a slightly off-key version of the record that had been playing on the jukebox when they entered the hall. *"Some enchanted evening, you will meet a stranger. You will meet a stranger, across a crowded room. . . ."*

In all her days, Eun-Me had never once seen anyone so strange as this man wearing an apron who could cook. She still had a lot to learn about Americans, even after living and working with them for many years. The thought of how her dinner might taste made her lips curl and her nose crinkle in disdain. She was anxious to see the look on Miss Jennifer's face when she discovered her dinner had been cooked by a man.

While she waited for her meal to be served, Eun-Me positioned herself beside *Sahmonim* at the end of a long table, in a spot where she could watch the door.

"Yum. Those fries smell wonderful." Miss Jennifer set her purse onto the table and plopped herself into a chair on the other side of *Sahmonim* Woods. "From the looks of our chef, he knows how to cook, and am I ever ready to eat some real food."

"I'm glad to see you're feeling better," *Sahmonim* replied. "Just be careful not to overdo too soon." She leaned toward Eun-Me and gave her a cheery smile. "Personally, I'd rather have a bowl of your bean paste soup."

Eun-Me decided then and there that she would never understand Miss Jennifer.

When "Sarge" set in front of her a paper-lined plastic basket brimming with the American-style fried potatoes and hamburger sandwich, Eun-Me bowed her head and thanked the Lord for the food, but she still hadn't mustered much of an appetite. Instead, her attentions were focused on the door, knowing she wouldn't be able to relax until Philip returned.

She pushed her picked-over supper away and sat up straight in her chair when the door finally opened. Although her heart sank briefly to see a uniformed American army officer standing in the doorway, she perked up again when Philip and *Moksanim* followed him into the room. With one look at their solemn expressions, Eun-Me knew the news wasn't good.

"Ladies. Gentlemen. If I might have a word with you?" The military man stood directly over Eun-Me while Philip and his father took the seats *Sahmonim* had reserved for them across from her. Above her head, Eun-Me heard the officer clear his throat, but he waited for everyone to quiet down before he began to speak. The Carroll boys, who sat with their parents at the other end of the long table, had been practicing their fencing skills with French fries, but they dropped their "swords" immediately when their father snapped his fingers.

"I'm Major Randolph Denton, and this small compound is under my command. I won't bother with pleasantries because I know you're all anxious to hear the latest news from Seoul. Let me get right to the point."

Eun-Me longed to turn and watch the major while he spoke. She didn't want to miss the meaning of any of this crucial announcement, but she didn't want to interrupt, so she focused her full attention on listening to his words instead.

"The South Korean troops have not succeeded in repelling the Communist forces as we'd hoped. In fact, the enemy is sweeping across the 38th parallel, pushing south at a rather alarming speed."

The clipped manner of his speech heightened Eun-Me's nervousness, and she could feel the muscles in her shoulders tense.

"Today, I received word that U.S. Ambassador Muccio has ordered the evacuation of all American civilians. The train station here in Daejon is already in a state of mass confusion, but we were able to send the local missionaries out on a Pusan-bound train. And more than five hundred of our fellow countrymen who reside in Seoul left this afternoon on a Norwegian fertilizer ship headed for Japan."

At any other time, she knew Philip would have made some joke about the vessel's cargo, but he still wore the same solemn expression she'd seen when he walked in the door.

"Before you begin to worry unduly, let me hasten to say that I believe we are far enough south of the fighting that we are in no immediate danger now, but we are prepared to transport all Americans to safety as soon as possible."

"All Americans to safety." That part of the message rang in her ears, leaving her to wonder what would become of a Korean girl like her.

seven

Eun-Me strained to concentrate on the rest of the major's speech, but worries over her own dilemma kept distracting her. She knew the Woods family would do everything in their power to protect her and keep her close to them, but from the way the major talked, the decision to stay in Korea or evacuate might no longer be up to them. She wasn't naïve enough to think that the U.S. military would show any consideration or concern for her. She'd be just one more homeless Korean refugee among the masses trying to flee the horrors of war.

From behind her, she heard the major say something about putting everyone up for the night and sending them out with a convoy headed for Taegu at 0600 tomorrow and onto Pusan by train from there. Did this mean that within hours—or minutes—she'd be put out on the streets, abandoned in a strange city? Eun-Me's heart pounded in her chest at the very real possibility. Even though she was an orphan, at least back in Seoul she had a home and a livelihood. Here she knew no one, and worst of all, she had no place to go amid the outbreak of war.

The sound of chairs scraping across the floor jarred her from her fretful reverie. The major was backing toward the door and motioning for them to come.

"If you'll follow me, I'll show you to a barracks so

you can catch a few hours' sleep. I wish we had better accommodations to offer you, but as tired as you all must be from your travels today, an army cot is likely to feel as good as any feather bed."

She slumped in her seat as the others moved to obey Major Denton's command. Philip came around from the other side of the table and tugged on the back of her chair. "Come on, Grace. I know you're exhausted, but you can't sleep here. Why don't you walk with me?"

"B–b–but, I'm not an American. The U.S. military won't take care of me." Hard as she tried to hold back her welling tears, they began to stream down each cheek and drip onto her lap. She buried her face in her hands, and her chest rose and fell with quick, quiet sobs.

"Please. Don't cry. I watched you while Major Denton spoke and I knew you were upset." Philip dropped to one knee next to her and drew his face so close that she could feel his breath on the back of her hand. "I'm not at liberty to divulge the reason right now, but I have it on full authority that you will be allowed to go with us when the convoy sets out for Taegu tomorrow at dawn. Trust me on this. I promise I'll explain everything once Dad has had a chance to talk with Mom."

She lowered her hands from her face just far enough to look at him, but he looked so blurry through her tears that she had to swipe at her eyes with her fingers before she could get a clear view of him. His eyes confirmed his sincerity.

She couldn't begin to guess what secret plan he and his father had plotted to grant her the privileges afforded the

Americans, but her gratitude knew no bounds. She wouldn't pry for any information until he was ready to share.

"Here. Let me loan you my hanky so you can dry your tears. You know I never could bear to see you cry." He stood and patted at all his pockets in search of his missing handkerchief. He had obviously forgotten that he'd loaned it to her in the truck earlier that afternoon. She withdrew the soiled linen from up her sleeve.

"Is this the one you're searching for?" She smiled through her sniffles as she dabbed at her remaining tears with the one corner of the handkerchief that was still fairly clean. Despite her added grime and tears, it still held the essence of Philip. Eun-Me inhaled a deep whiff and held her breath. She wanted to keep the cloth forever, dirt and all, as a memento of today. She may have a precious few such days left to spend together with him.

A light rain had begun to fall when they caught up with the others. They tagged onto the tail end of their processional and filed past Major Denton into the barracks that he had assigned to them for the night. Not a single one of the Americans bothered to leave their shoes at the door, so Eun-Me reluctantly followed suit and kept her street shoes on as she walked across the concrete floor.

The Quonset hut's one large room, devoid of any decoration, caught Eun-Me off guard. She hadn't expected to share sleeping quarters with the men, but the major made no mention of a separate facility for the women.

Other than the canvas army cots that lined both the walls, no other furniture occupied the room. At the end of each cot, a stripe-ticked pillow sat atop a neatly folded blanket. The blanket's olive green wool looked scratchy and uncomfortable, and Eun-Me didn't share Michael and Caleb's enthusiasm for the idea of sleeping like real-live army men. She longed for the thick softness of her *yoh*.

Miss Jennifer had already shaken out a blanket and collapsed onto one of the beds. By all appearances, she had fallen asleep fully clothed, right down to her shoes.

"You'll find the showers and latrine out back. Like I said, I wish I could offer you something a bit more comfortable, but at least you'll be out of the elements for the night." Major Denton peered out the doorway and into the night sky. "More rain's moving in. These monsoons may be great for the rice crops, but they wreck havoc on the roads. You may be in for a rough go tomorrow, and reveille will sound before dawn, so I'd advise lights-out right away."

"You've been most accommodating, Major." Professor Spencer thrust out his hand as he stepped forward from the ring of missionaries that had formed around the officer. "Thank you for all your help."

The others added a hearty, "Amen."

Eun-Me ached from head to toe, so while all the men left to bring in the knapsacks, she decided to lie down on the cot next to Miss Jennifer and wait for them to return. She told herself that she would only rest her eyes for a minute or two, then she'd shower and shake out her dusty clothes before putting them back on again.

❧

"Philip. Son. I hate to do this to you, but you've got to get up."

"What? What is it? Did you find Grace?" Philip bolted upright on his cot when his father's voice and gentle shaking broke into his nightmare. The dream was a repeat of one he'd had a few days earlier—running from a tiger in the woods. But this time, he'd lost Grace and not his grandmother's ring.

"You must have been dreaming." His father gave him a comforting pat on the back as if he were still a little boy. "Grace is still sleeping soundly on her cot right next to Jennifer." For a quick second, he cast the beam of the flashlight he carried to illuminate their sleeping forms. "I don't believe either of them has budged one iota since they fell asleep three hours ago. However, thanks to Kim Il Sung's army, they won't get to sleep much longer. We've had a change of plans. Major Denton wants us all to assemble at the mess hall immediately, and you're to be ready to evacuate."

"What time is it? Did I sleep through reveille?" Philip looked for signs of daybreak coming through one of the narrow windows, but blackness was all he could see. He thought that perhaps the heavy rain, which pounded on the sheet metal roof with a deafening clamor, prevented any sunlight from shining into the room.

"No. According to my watch, the time is just a few minutes after midnight. However, a reconnaissance team pulled in a few minutes ago, and they've heard reports that the invading troops from the north may reach Daejon as early as morning's light. To make matters worse, all this rain caused a rockslide near Okchon, rendering the highway to Taegu impassable from here. If y'all expect to get south before the back roads are cut off, you're going to have to leave as soon as we can get you out of here. I'll waken the others in a minute, but I wanted a chance to speak with you first." The soft glow from the flashlight cast long shadows against his father's face and made him appear very old.

"Guess this means there'll be no turning back in my decision to stay on as an interpreter until they can get their own men in here. I'd make Dick Spencer stay with me if he hadn't limited his Korean vocabulary to theology. If I get my hands on one Lieutenant Rusty Barnard, I just might strangle him for sending word to the major about my so-called 'excellent language skills.' With friends like him, who needs. . .oh, never mind." Philip knew that his father took the recommendation as a high compliment, despite the empty threat and mock stern tone of his words.

"Your mother agrees with me, though. I owe our beloved Korea my best efforts to bring peace back to our land. And if by staying to help with negotiations, I can play a part in insuring Grace's safety. . ." His dad had to clear his throat before he could finish his thought. "Well, you know I'd lay down my life for that dear girl."

He shuffled a large manila envelope from under one arm to the next. The beam of his flashlight danced across the floor as he reached for his back pocket and withdrew his billfold. "I've carried this business card around in my wallet for a couple months. Kept meaning to take it out but always forgot. I guess the Lord knew we'd need it to-day." Philip accepted the card from his dad, who pointed his flashlight to illuminate the words.

"This has the address and phone number of an old friend

by the name of Tanaka. Tanaka *Sen-sei* in Japanese, but he prefers that you use the Korean title, *Hwangjangnim,* instead. I want you to contact him as soon as you get to Japan. He'll take good care of you. I don't know if you remember him, but he and his wife came from Japan some fifty years ago to open an orphanage in Seoul. He had to return to his homeland during the war, but by then they were both more Korean at heart than Japanese. I saw him just a couple of months ago. He was back in Seoul for a few days in order to bury his beloved mate. As her last request, she asked to be buried in the foreigners' cemetery. That's a story for another day, but after the memorial service, he said if I or my family ever had occasion to pass through Beppu, the coastal town where he lives, we'd have a place to stay. Beppu is the closest Japanese port from Pusan. You'll probably drop anchor there. After you leave for San Francisco with Jennifer, I am confident he'll watch after your mother and Grace until I can travel over to bring them home."

Philip watched his dad pull the manila envelope from under his arm and offer it to him.

"The major kept his end of the bargain we struck when we met with him. Here are the U.S. military pass and identification documents he had promised to prepare for Grace. But I'd still feel better about her safety if you were to stick close beside her until you arrive in Japan. Folks are liable to get desperate if this war continues to escalate. Grace may be in danger if the knowledge of these special papers and permits were to fall into the wrong hands."

His father leaned in close and whispered into Philip's

good ear. "I've been watching you the last few days. I don't think you'll find the task of sticking close to Grace too difficult a chore. I'm glad to see the two of you have picked up your close friendship where you left off back in '42. She's needed a confidante and since we're the 'big bosses' now, she's too tied to convention to confide much in your mother or me. Grace has done your heart some good, too, I do believe."

Philip felt ill at ease to learn that he and Grace had been under his parent's scrutiny. Or maybe his discomfort came from knowing his dad had hit the nail on the head. The very mention of her name sent a warm happiness flooding over him. He swung his feet over the side of his cot and donned his shoes, then stood.

"You can count on me to take good care of all the womenfolk, Dad. I just wish I didn't have to say good-bye to you so soon."

"I understand the necessity of getting Jennifer back to San Francisco. And who knows how long I'll be deterred here. I'm certain we'll see the Lord's hand in all of this someday. But, Son, if I don't get another opportunity to say so, I want you to know I'm proud of you. I'm praying that God will protect us all until the day that you're back in Korea and we're working together for Him on the same team."

Philip's father threw his arms around him, and they pounded each other on the back in a bear hug. "Well, we'd better shake the others out of bed. I want you to put as many miles as possible between you and the Communists." With a final slap on the back, his dad stepped back and handed him the flashlight. "I hereby bestow on you the honor of waking

Cinderella and Sleeping Beauty over there."

Guided by the flickering luminescence of the dying flashlight, Philip crossed the room and paused between the two
cots where Grace and Jennifer slept. His head volleyed
back and forth as he contemplated which of the women he
should waken first.

Jennifer slept with her mouth open. All traces of lipstick
had long ago been wiped clean. A trickle of drool trailed
down her pale, gaunt cheek and into her blond hair.

Pity welled within him, and Philip wondered what had
ever attracted him to her. Any beauty she possessed seemed
so superficial compared to Grace. And he didn't mean just
the effects of cosmetics on her outward appearance.

As he thought about his relationship with Jennifer, he
realized the stormy end to their engagement had been brew-
ing for many months. He'd simply chosen to be blind rather
than read the warning signs.

Even though she'd been faithful in attending church
with him, whenever he had tried to draw her into a time of
prayer or Bible study, she always had something "important" to do. She seemed more concerned about planning a
fancy church wedding featuring the beautiful bride than in
building the foundations of a Christ-centered marriage.
Life revolved around *her*—not *them*.

Yet, he had to accept a good portion of the blame and
not be so quick to judge Jennifer. He'd been wrong to try
and force his call to ministry on her or assume that if he
could just get her over here, she'd have a change of heart.
Jennifer couldn't help her self-serving attitudes and self-
centered disposition. An indulgent heritage and egocentric

environment were hard to overcome. The undertow of materialism had nearly sucked him in as well.

Grace, on the other hand. . . Her face radiated an inner peace even while she slept. She had chosen to allow God to strengthen her character through the tragedies of life rather than become embittered and sad.

Wisps of raven hair had come loose from her braid and blown across her face. Philip bent to lightly brush the wayward strands back into place. At the feather-soft sensation of her skin against his fingertips, he felt compelled to caress her forehead again. Her eyes flew open and she gave him the most enchanting smile he'd ever seen. He felt certain his heart stopped beating for a brief moment or two. The look they shared implied more than a trade of neighborly affection between two old friends.

Oh, dear Lord, Philip prayed in silent desperation, *don't let me break this wonderful woman's heart. No good can possibly come by encouraging these romantic feelings I have for her. We are worlds apart in every way.*

Jennifer's sniveling effectively broke the sweet tension he and Grace had just exchanged. "Dr. Woods. Whatever has possessed you to go stomping around in the middle of the night and scaring me half to death? I don't know about *her,* but I, for one, need my beauty sleep."

Philip gritted his teeth. Not so long ago, he had considered marrying this woman. Now he had to force himself to even be civil to her. "Put a sock in it, Jennifer," he grumbled. "I'm not doing this for my health."

❧

Eun-Me clutched the packet that bore her name and the

official seal of the U.S. Army tightly to her chest as she prepared to go out into the midnight rain. She had argued that she couldn't possibly accept these documents, knowing what *Moksanim* Woods had promised in exchange. Yet *Moksanim* refused to listen to her and had insisted that he would stay no matter what. He assured her that the Lord had chosen this way to work all things together for her good.

Sahmonim stayed behind in the mess hall with *Moksanim* for a time of private good-byes while the others proceeded to their assigned vehicles. As if providing Eun-Me with travel passes weren't enough, Major Denton had arranged for his personal driver to transport Eun-Me in his jeep, along with *Sahmonim* Woods, Philip, and Miss Jennifer. All the others had to climb into the back of a troop transport truck for the trip to Taegu.

However, they hadn't traveled very far until a fresh wave of overwhelming weariness transplanted any feelings Eun-Me had of preferential treatment. They took so many twists and turns around the dark, mountainous countryside that their arduous journey from Taechon Beach the day before seemed like a Sunday afternoon joyride now. And this time, she didn't have her previous pleasure of sitting next to Philip and exchanging clandestine smiles. Instead, she had wedged herself in between *Sahmonim* and Miss Jennifer. The soldier who was driving offered only his name and rank when Philip tried to speak to him. Corporal David Frye made it clear that his job involved transporting them to Taegu. Any conversation was optional. His silence set the precedent for the duration of their nighttime ride.

Occasionally, Eun-Me heard *Sahmonim*'s soft humming of a favorite hymn, but only slow and steady breathing came from Miss Jennifer.

Torrential monsoon rains followed them from the time they left the compound and the open sides and convertible top covering the jeep provided them with little protection from the elements. Eun-Me felt wet all the way down to her bones.

The darkness of night merely served to amplify her fears. She held her breath at every bend in the road, watching nervously behind them to make certain that the other vehicles in the convoy stayed in her view, terrified to watch the road ahead for fear that the Communists would pop out from behind some rock and ambush them. Such a choke hold of terror gripped her at times, she thought she might scream if they didn't arrive at their destination soon.

She kept herself from breaking down by focusing her gaze on the silhouette of Philip's face outlined by the dashboard lights. As long as he sat in front of her, she knew she could survive.

Then, as if Someone shut the spigot off, the rain stopped. Morning's first light split the black horizon with glorious brilliance. And Eun-Me offered spontaneous praise to the Lord for seeing them safely through the night.

Beside her, Miss Jennifer squirmed in her seat and twisted her head to look out the window. "That has to go on record as the longest night in history. Are we getting close yet? I've got the most awful crick in my neck."

She hadn't asked the question of anyone in particular, and Philip showed no signs of answering her, so for the first time since they'd left the Daejon KMAG compound, Corporal Frye spoke.

"By my estimation, we should be pulling into Taegu in another hour or so." He shot a quick glance in his rearview mirror at Miss Jennifer and his voice brightened considerably, as though he'd just noticed his pretty passenger for the very first time. "But if you need me to, we can pull over and let you stretch your legs by the side of the road. Even better, I know of a roadside *shik-tang* up ahead where we can grab a bite of breakfast if you don't mind Korean food."

"I could really go for a bowl of that yummy sticky rice. Dr. Woods, you don't mind if we stop, do you?"

Philip swiveled in his seat. His mouth dropped open and he stared wide-eyed at Miss Jennifer. "N–no. I don't mind. I'm always ready to eat, but we ought to ask the others. They may be anxious to get right to the train station. We can pick up something to eat there. Mom. Grace. What do you gals prefer?"

Eun-Me absentmindedly nodded her head in support of *Sahmonim*'s, "Sure, let's stop." Her mind was busy trying to figure out what had brought about the change in Miss Jennifer's opinion toward Korean food. She didn't want to be judgmental, but she suspected that the remark wasn't purely innocent. Had she intended to poke fun at her? Or was she trying to stir up jealousy in Philip by acting flirtatious with another man? In either case, Eun-Me didn't think Miss Jennifer had achieved the desired effect. She no longer cared one whit about what Philip's old girlfriend thought of her, and Philip didn't seem to show any signs of jealousy. Instead, he turned his attentions to her, not Jennifer.

"I'm going to order you a cup of ginseng tea and make sure you eat a big breakfast. I know you hardly touched your dinner last night, and there's no telling how many days we'll have to travel before we make it to Japan." Eun-Me felt her cheeks warm under his close examination.

❧

"That tea looks and smells just like dirt. How can you drink that stuff?" Rather than taking offense at Miss Jennifer's remark, this time Eun-Me covered her mouth with her hand and chuckled aloud. Then she put the cup to her lips and finished the last earthy dregs of her ginseng tea.

"I personally don't like the taste, but ginseng's good for your health. Are you certain you won't try just a spot?" Eun-Me pretended to tip the pot toward Miss Jennifer's cup.

"No, no. That's quite all right, but thank you. I'm feeling just fine this morning. There's not a thing wrong with my health."

Another round of laughter rippled across the foreigners. From the moment they had entered the roadside *shik-tang* to eat breakfast, Miss Jennifer had entertained everyone, beginning by making fun of herself as she attempted to sit on the floor Korean-style. This was a side of Miss Jennifer's personality that Eun-Me had not seen until now. Eun-Me could understand how Philip might have fallen in love with *this* Miss Jennifer—delightful and witty and at ease in a crowd. Could the bitter remarks and crotchety disposition displayed by Miss Jennifer all week simply be due to her not feeling well? If so, and the true Miss Jennifer had shown herself again, then Philip would soon be racing to make up with her.

The thought occurred to Eun-Me that her tender exchanges with Philip may have come to an end. Suddenly, she no longer felt enthralled by this new Miss Jennifer. She cast an inquiring glance across the table toward Philip. Like the others, he was watching Miss Jennifer, yet he did not appear to be wooed by her charm. Instead, he eyed her suspiciously.

Even so, Eun-Me felt certain that their inevitable reunion was just a matter of time.

From the far end of the table, where the three military drivers had been entertaining the Carroll boys, Corporal Frye cleared his throat and tapped lightly on his teacup with a metal chopstick. At the signal, everyone looked his way. "I think we'd better load up again and hit the road. We've been stopped way too long." He stole a quick peek at his watch. "Major's orders were to deliver you all directly to the Taegu train depot."

The long-legged Americans untwisted themselves from their awkward positions on the floor, settled up their bill with the proprietor, and headed out the door. The breakfast and the morning's frivolity had invigorated the group at a critical time and, as they climbed back in the jeep and trucks, most of them seemed in good spirits and ready to endure the remainder of their trip to Taegu.

Miss Jennifer hooked her arm through *Sahmonim* Woods's, and they walked together toward the jeep. Walking alone, Eun-Me started to follow them across the dirt-packed yard of the *shik-tang,* but she paused when Philip called, "Grace. Wait up."

As he fell into step beside her, Eun-Me crooked her

neck to look at Philip and caught him staring after Miss Jennifer. Her heart sank.

"She's the life of the party when she wants to be."

Eun-Me managed to squeak an "Um-hum" through her emotion-clogged throat, but even if she could have thought of a more detailed response, she would have choked on her words.

"I hope and pray this is the Jennifer who shows up on the boat when we leave Japan headed for San Francisco. My trip might be bearable, if so."

This time, Eun-Me couldn't even choke out a monosyllable reply, and Philip stopped in his tracks the second he looked at her.

"Grace, are you all right? Did I put my foot in my mouth again?"

His foot was nowhere near his mouth, so Eun-Me assumed the comment to be another unfamiliar American idiom. The time that she spent pondering the phrase took her mind off her faltering emotions just long enough for her to regain sufficient composure to speak. "I'm fine. Really. Don't pay any attention to me. I was just thinking about how 'topsy-turvy' everything has turned, as *Sahmonim* would say. Once again, life proves to be totally unpredictable."

"Yes. Life and Jennifer Anderson."

Eun-Me could feel Philip looking at her as though he wanted to say something more, but she avoided his gaze and quickened her pace. "I'd better hurry. *Sahmonim* has already climbed into the jeep, and Miss Jennifer is waiting for me to sit in the middle so she can take her seat."

The corporal kept the jeep's speed at a crawl until the

other two vehicles clattered up onto the paved road behind them. Even then, his feet kept tapping the brakes and working the clutch in an attempt to dodge the people walking alongside and down the middle of the street.

As Eun-Me expected on any given morning at this hour, some of the pedestrians appeared to be typical provincial citizens going about their daily routines. Yet, unlike most mornings, refugees comprised most of this throng. The women carried all of their worldly possessions tied in big bundles and perched on top of their heads. The children, clutching onto a sibling's hand, raced their feet in double-time to keep stride with their parents. Rice-filled gunnysacks were slung over the shoulders of many of the men.

Since Philip's transistor radio first crackled with the initial invasion reports, this surreal scene of commonplace mixed with chaos personified for Eun-Me the terrifying reality of an approaching war.

When their convoy reached the outskirts of Taegu, Eun-Me thought she heard music. She looked through the front windshield to see uniformed schoolchildren lining both sides of the road. They waved Korean flags high above their heads. Their young soprano voices surrounded them, and the strains of Korea's national anthem filled the air.

Tears fell unimpeded down Eun-Me's face as she joined in singing the melody. When she reached the chorus, she could no longer find voice to repeat the words, so she hummed along. And sobbed.

Sahmonim leaned across Eun-Me's back and began to whisper a translation of the lyrics for Jennifer:

Until the East Sea's waves are dry and Paektu
  Mountain worn away,
God watch o'er our land forever! Our Korea we stand
  and cheer!

Rose of Sharon, thousand miles and range and river
  land!
Guarded by her people, ever may Korea stand!

However, at the last verse, *Sahmonim*, too, had to pause
and swallow her tears before she could continue.

With such a will; such a spirit, loyalty, heart and
  hand,
Let us love, come grief, come gladness,
This our beloved land!

eight

Tuesday, June 27, 1950

Philip raked his fingers through the front of his hair in an attempt to mask his own moist eyes. Even while he watched the scene unfold, he knew that he would look back on this moment as a pivotal point in his life. His soul welled with pride at the thought that these people were his people. This land was his land.

Only one overriding motivation kept him pressing toward America instead of staying here with his father to work for peace. He knew he had to complete his residency so that when he returned, he'd be fully qualified to serve the Korean people and fulfill God's call. No matter what the future held in store for Korea, he vowed that he'd be back to his adopted motherland someday.

Grace's cries filtered up from the rear seat. He longed to hold her in his arms and comfort her. She had looked so distressed back at the *shik-tang*.

He worried that he had upset her by bringing up the fact that he would soon be going on to San Francisco with Jennifer and leaving Grace and his mother alone. After all, the realization must be sinking in that within a matter of hours, she would be leaving Korea and going to Japan.

He shook his head, disgusted with himself for his insensitivity. His petty problems with Jennifer paled when compared to the ordeals facing Grace.

Given how she struggled with feelings of bitterness toward the Japanese, the prospect of finding herself surrounded by the lifelong enemies who had killed her father and brother, with no way home, may be almost as terrifying as the invasion of the Korean Communists from the north.

He buried his head in his hands. This time, not to hide a few tears, but to bring to the Lord his mental list of prayer requests: Grace, his father, his mother, traveling mercies to Japan, Jennifer's safe transport home. Then, his prayers went back to Grace again.

"Sir, we're nearing the Taegu train depot, but I'm worried about dropping you off in the middle of this mob." The corporal's tight grip on the steering wheel made his knuckles deathly white, and Philip realized they hadn't moved in traffic for quite some time. "I don't see how a group of your size could possibly all stay together. Any suggestions as to what I should do?"

Philip scanned the sea of black, bobbing heads that moved with tsunami force toward the station's row of ticket windows. "We don't appear to be going anywhere fast. Let me jog back to the transport truck and poll the other men. Wait right here." He meant the remark as a wisecrack, knowing they weren't likely to budge, but the pinch-lipped Corporal Frye gave a quick nod and kept his eyes peeled on the road.

He eased himself out of the jeep and began to wedge and push his way upstream against the shoving crowd toward the truck.

❦

"Isn't there a special station for Americans?" Eun-Me jumped at the touch of Miss Jennifer's hand on her arm when she leaned forward to address their driver. Her emerald eyes sparkled and grew rounder with fear, darting in every direction as she scanned the pressing crowd. "I've never seen so many people in one place in my life. We'll be crushed to death for sure."

"You'll be fine, Dear," *Sahmonim* reached across Eun-Me to offer a calming pat to Miss Jennifer's knee. "Such crowds aren't all that unusual in Seoul, and I've always survived. You've got one big advantage over these folks. With your height, you'll stand head and shoulders above the rest. Thank goodness the rain has stopped or we'd have to fight to keep the umbrella spokes from poking out our eyes. Let me offer one suggestion, though." *Sahmonim* shot a quick glance at the corporal, then leaned in farther, and lowered her voice to a raspy whisper. "Tuck your passport and any cash you might be carrying down in your underwear. Pickpockets thrive on situations like this."

Eun-Me recalled the skimpy underthings she'd packed for Miss Jennifer, and she didn't think that her foundation garments could provide sufficient support for such a task, but she kept her opinion to herself.

"Thanks for the advice, but I'm wearing a money belt. I should be fine on that front."

While Eun-Me still wore the same clothes she had on the day before, Miss Jennifer had postponed their departure from the compound an extra fifteen minutes so that she could change. The black flared skirt of her two-piece traveling suit could very easily hide such a bulge. Perhaps Miss Jennifer's decision to wear a skirt on their evacuation journey, rather than her form-fitting dungarees, was not as illogical as Eun-Me had originally thought. Of course, she would have no trouble hiding her packet of documents down a wide leg of her *mom-pei* pants, and she had no money to worry about.

In a flurry of movement, Philip shoved their knapsacks and Miss Jennifer's beach bag into the jeep's floorboard ahead of him, then jumped back into his seat. A spike of sandy blond hair stood straight out from the crown of his head, and the collar of his shirt had flipped up on one side. His disheveled appearance seemed to bother no one else but her, so Eun-Me fought the urge to set him right again.

"Looks like this is where we'll say, 'Good-bye,' Corporal Frye," Philip said as they exchanged a handshake. "The consensus reached after my quick powwow with the other men is that we'll stand a better chance of getting tickets on the train if we split up and queue in different lines. We've decided to all go our separate ways from here."

Eun-Me caught sight of the pale-skinned and light-haired Carroll family before they were swallowed up in the jostling swarm. Each parent clutched a boy in one arm and yanked their duffel bag between them with their free hands.

"The Carrolls said to tell you folks that they hope to see you on the train." Professor Spencer stuck his head in the jeep's open doorway on the passenger side. "Reverend and Mrs. Taylor have already taken off, too. But, just in case we don't connect again, I wanted to wish you all Godspeed. Mrs. Woods, Grace, I'll see you back in Seoul as soon as this nasty mess is settled, if not before. Philip, don't let this experience keep you from visiting your folks again soon. You hear? Glad to have met you, Jennifer." He waved in salutation, then was gone, his balding head floating on top of the wave of humanity.

"Okay, ladies. No sense postponing this any longer. Have you secured all your valuables?" Philip waited until he heard a distinct, "Yes," from each one before handing them their respective bags.

"Pay attention, Jennifer. The minute you set foot out of the jeep, I want you to get between Grace and my mom and lock your arms in theirs to form a human chain. Don't let go for anything. No arguments."

If Miss Jennifer had been inclined to protest, she wouldn't have dared after the steely glare Philip shot at her. Eun-Me squirmed in her seat when his focus shifted toward her, but his scowl lifted into the slightest of smiles when their eyes met.

"Grace, since you're the only Korean among us, you'd be the most likely one to get lost in this crowd, so I'm going to hold your hand and keep you close to me while I lead the way. We aren't going to worry about what people think." Her face warmed to know he had read her mind yet another time, and she dropped her gaze away from his clairvoyant stare.

"Are we ready?" He didn't wait for a response, but jumped out and offered his hand while first Miss Jennifer, then Eun-Me climbed from the back of the jeep, followed by *Sahmonim*.

Before Eun-Me could plant both her feet on the ground, Miss Jennifer had looped her straw bag onto the crook of her elbow and locked arms with her. Philip, upon seeing Eun-Me struggle with one free arm to adjust her own pack, bent down and murmured in her ear, "I'd say she's taken my instruction a bit too seriously. Let me help you with that." He slipped her arm through the cloth ties of her knapsack and pushed the bundle up onto her shoulder, then he offered his open hand.

He engulfed her tiny palm in his and intertwined their fingers, finalizing the act with a soft squeeze. Eun-Me allowed herself to be pulled into the current of refugees with Miss Jennifer and *Sahmonim* in tow. She paid no attention to the strangers pressing in on her. She felt only the tingling touch of her hand wrapped securely in his. She would gladly follow Philip to the ends of the earth if he did this the entire way.

"Thief! Stop! I've been robbed!" Eun-Me's ears rang from Miss Jennifer's piercing screams. Philip immediately stopped their processional and spun around. She still clutched Eun-Me in a vice-grip, but from the crook of Miss Jennifer's arm, where her straw beach bag had hung moments before, now only the strap dangled in the breeze.

In vain, Eun-Me surveyed the crowd around them in search of the thief. Any purse-snatcher or pickpocket with the skill to go unnoticed while cutting a swaying bag from someone's arm stood a good chance of making a clean getaway.

Philip pulled the strap away and examined Miss Jennifer's arm for any signs of injury. "You don't appear hurt, so we need to keep moving."

He tugged Eun-Me's hand and took a step, but Miss Jennifer refused to budge. Eun-Me, caught in the middle, stretched in both directions.

"You've got to call the police so they can catch the dirty pilferer." Miss Jennifer no longer displayed any signs of her early morning good humor.

"Just forget it, Jennifer. We have to hurry."

"I need my stuff." She growled at Philip with an angry snarl. "It's bad enough that I had to leave most of it behind in the broken car, but now all I've got is what I'm wearing!"

"Jennifer, we're in the middle of a war. The police aren't about to drop what they're doing because some rich American lost her pajamas. If there's time, we'll try to buy you a new toothbrush when we get to Pusan. We'll figure out the rest later. But, please. Let's go."

Eun-Me ran through a mental inventory of the things in her knapsack. She didn't think she possessed a single item that would interest Miss Jennifer. Not here or at home in Seoul.

People shoved and prodded their way toward the ticket windows. No one bothered to stand in a line. The only rule that applied in this cacophony seemed to be, "He who shoves hardest wins." Philip gave up on being polite after a dozen or more stooped *halmonims* cut in front of him. "If that's the way they want to play, watch this," he mumbled at Eun-Me. And he wormed them through to the ticket clerk.

"Pusan gachee sae-jang chusaeyo." As Philip stated his request for the tickets, Eun-Me noted with pride that his accent remained perfect after all these years.

The man behind the counter didn't even look up when he replied, *"Opsumnida."*

"What did he say?" Miss Jennifer shouted to Eun-Me over the din.

"He said the tickets to Pusan are sold out."

Without saying a word, Philip pulled back the *won* he'd shoved into the slot beneath the window bars and added a crisp American ten-dollar bill on top of the Korean currency. The clerk finally raised his head. A second later,

Philip stepped back from the window with four tickets squeezed in his left hand.

They snaked their way from the plaza area and through the turnstiles onto the platform to wait for the next southbound train. Philip led their cadre to a remote corner of the depot and away from prying onlookers. He dropped Eun-Me's hand and motioned them into a huddle.

"In case we get separated, I want us each to carry our own ticket." Philip handed one to each of the women and slipped his inside his shirt pocket. "Mom, you're in charge of making sure Jennifer never leaves your side. You, Grace, and I can get to Pusan by ourselves if we have to, but she's totally dependent on us."

Even now, away from the teaming masses, Miss Jennifer held tight to the sleeves of Eun-Me and *Sahmonim*. Philip's words made her pinch a bit harder.

"If one of us misses this train, I think the others should go on to Pusan and wait. We'll rendezvous at the taxi stand in front of the train station. If two trains come in and the missing party still hasn't arrived, then go to our nearest church and ask the pastor to put you up for the night. We'll catch up with one another there."

In the distance, a breathy train whistle started low and rose to a shrill crescendo. The piercing blast sent all the waiting passengers scurrying for a post near the edge of the platform as a cloud of soot darkened the morning sky.

"Okay. Here she comes." Philip, clutching Eun-Me's hand, waded into the throng once more. "The ten o'clock southbound is only forty-five minutes late. Mom, you and Jennifer go ahead of us so we're certain you get on board."

Miss Jennifer released her grip on Eun-Me to cling onto

Sahmonim with both hands while the drab green train bellowed into the station and chugged to a stop. From what Eun-Me could count where she stood, she estimated the rail engine pulled eight cars—each filled to capacity.

Everyone converged at the landings in front of each car door to wait for the porters to open the floodgates and admit new passengers. Philip stood at Eun-Me's side, clasping her hand painfully tight. The prodding and jostling intensified, propelling Eun-Me into *Sahmonim*'s back with such force that she thought she might suffocate if she couldn't catch a breath soon.

No one in front of them seemed willing to allow this car's lone departing passenger off the train, lest they lose their hard-earned position. The porter resorted to kicking into the barricade of bodies to punch out an opening large enough for passage of the young *omma* with a baby tied to her back.

Once his charge had left the train, the porter stepped back and permitted the melee to resume in the push to board. Eun-Me felt her feet leave the floor, and sheer momentum carried her toward the small opening.

Ahead of her, she watched *Sahmonim* and Miss Jennifer step, as one body, over the threshold onto the train. Eun-Me released her hold on Philip and reached out to grab the railing on either side of the door to pull herself on board. Before she could snatch a firm hold, two middle-aged men pushed their way in front of her.

Eun-Me fished for the railing again, but felt only air.

The train pitched forward to signal its imminent departure, and the press of the crowd eased. Suddenly left without support, Eun-Me began to flail her arms in every direction, searching for something—anything—to hold onto that might steady her teetering balance. The train began to roll.

A rising sense of panic sent a squeak of fright from her lips as her leg slipped into the crevice between the platform and the locomotive. From the corner of her eye, she saw Philip reaching out for her, but he couldn't catch her in time.

She fell forward, hitting the platform with her open palms. Her knapsack slipped off her shoulder and laid by her hands on the floor. Her right leg still dangled dangerously close to the lurching train. At the screeching blast of the train's whistle, Eun-Me froze.

Before she could think what to do, Philip reached under her arms and yanked her to her feet. He tugged a bit too hard and they both stumbled this time. But he quickly regained his balance, retrieved her knapsack, then steadied Eun-Me by wrapping her in his arms. Philip stepped backward, drawing her away from the platform, as the train increased its speed.

"Dr. Woods, Grace!" Caleb Carroll waved to them from the departing caboose. "We're goin' to Pusan!"

Eun-Me leaned into Philip's embrace, and together they watched the train shrink on the horizon, then disappear around a curve.

❦

"You're bleeding, Grace. Let me see your hands." Ignoring the quizzical stares of the Koreans who waited for the next train, Philip sat their bags at his feet and wove one leg through the straps. He turned Grace to face him and pulled her forward until she was between his knees. Then, he lifted her palms to examine them.

"Are you hurt anywhere else? How about your leg? Is it painful to put weight on it? Do I need to examine you for a break or a sprain?" She responded to each question with a quick shake of her head.

He stopped talking long enough to blow the loose dirt away from her open wounds.

As a doctor, he knew he shouldn't feel this way, but his hands were trembling. He decided he still hadn't recovered from the scare Grace had given him.

"Someone borrowed my handkerchief and I never got it back, or I'd already have you fixed up as good as new." Philip gave her a quick wink and grinned, then he began to blow again, this time caressing her delicate fingers with his thumbs. He hated to think of the hard labor that such dainty hands had been forced to do.

Without thinking, he raised her hands and gently kissed each tiny fingertip. Her hands started trembling, like his own had been doing since he first reached for her. "What are you doing. . . ?" Her voice trailed. But she didn't pull away.

A cold shiver raced through him at the thought of the tragedy that had nearly occurred. He'd come so close to losing his beautiful Grace, not briefly in the crowd, but to death beneath the iron wheels of the train. He circled her dainty wrists in his hands and guided her arms around his waist to wrap himself in her embrace. Releasing her hands, he reached his arms around her and pulled her close to him. Philip longed to keep her there forever, safe from harm.

He bent down and began to search her onyx eyes, unsure if they glistened with the vestiges of fear or the seeds of the same overpowering force that now drew him to her. Philip lifted his hand to stroke the outline of her cheek. Then, tipping her chin, he gently raised her face toward his.

There in the middle of the Taegu train station, jostled by the never-ending stream of travelers, he lowered his mouth to hers. Drawn to the softness of her quivering lips, he kissed her with all the love in his heart.

A whistle's sharp blast severed the fragile moment and brought Philip back to the reality of where they were. He could feel the renewed press of the crowd as they rushed to catch the approaching train. Grace dropped her arms and he loosened his hold on her, effectively completing the break.

He cleared his throat, trying to ignore the awkward silence that hung between them. His mind raced to find the appropriate words to explain or defend what had just occurred.

Philip desperately wanted to tell her that he loved her. Her response confirmed in his heart the fact that he had suspected for a long time. Yet, he couldn't bring himself to admit his love out loud. He would be gone from Korea for at least another three years. She deserved more than a long-distance love. Regardless, he didn't have time to make sense of it now. Another southbound train was pulling into the station, and he had to get them on board.

He looked down at the petite form of Grace. The top of her head came only as high as his chest. Philip took one more glance toward the slowing train and the sea of black heads pushing past them.

"Let's go," he said, and without waiting for her to approve of what he was about to do, he slung their bags over his shoulder and scooped her into his arms.

"Quick. Wrap your legs around me. I won't let you fall."

He had shamed her sufficiently by kissing her in public. If it meant seeing Grace safely onto that train, he would gladly breech this bit of decorum as well.

In a flash, Philip boosted her up and held her like a large child. Clutching her tightly with his right arm, he used his left as a battering ram to push his way forward to the open doorway of the railcar.

❧

Eun-Me hardly noticed her skinned hands and bruised knee, for her lips still burned with the tender pressure of Philip's kiss. That much-dreamed-of experience was all she'd imagined—and more. She would savor the sweet memory for all eternity.

Despite her desire to remain in his arms, now that he had carried her safely aboard the train, she knew the inevitable moment had come when she must release her hold on him.

"We've created enough of a stir. You'd better put me down now." She loosened her grasp and eased her feet to the ground.

In the short span of time Philip had taken to push their way on board, the train had filled to standing-room-only capacity. They jockeyed for a place to stand where they wouldn't get trampled by the rushing current of oncoming passengers. With her face still buried in his chest, they shuffled together, wedging themselves into a small space between the last seat and the back wall of the car.

Eun-Me had been surprised to see another locomotive arrive so soon after the other had departed, until she overheard the porter who stood guard at the door behind her explain the reason to another puzzled traveler. From what she could gather as the onslaught of riders pushed their way past, the railroad authorities had pressed into service every available locomotive to try and accommodate, while they could, the urgent demands of the evacuees flooding south.

After a couple of jerking false starts that bounced Eun-Me's head into Philip's chest, the train started to move. The porter used his shoulder to force the door closed against the tide of people still trying to board. Eun-Me looked out the window to see a handful of men so desperate to flee that they were climbing onto the roof of the train to ride. She breathed a prayer of thankfulness that Philip had gotten them inside.

Eun-Me lifted her head up toward him, and he offered a thin smile in return. This wasn't the time or place to discuss what had happened just moments before. She wasn't sure she could have found the words to express her feelings for him, even if they had been all alone. Nor was she sure if she could bear to hear Philip's explanation for what had occurred. She wanted to believe that he'd kissed her as an expression of his true love, but she feared the real reason stemmed from his being overcome with emotion after the heroic rescue he'd performed.

She was almost glad the circumstances wouldn't allow the truth to come out right now. She wanted to hold onto her fantasy as long as she could and believe that he loved her as much as she loved him.

Eun-Me relaxed as the clacking of the iron wheels played their unique lullaby. Her knees suddenly felt so weak that she might have collapsed to the floor if there'd been room to move. She could have easily dozed as she stood, for the catastrophic events of the past few days and minutes were beginning to take their toll on her. But she refused to succumb to sleep.

By this most recent twist to the week's cataclysmic turn of events, for the next several hours she'd been thrust into Philip's arms. She planned to savor each second; preserve each moment in her memory. She knew that each mile they traveled brought her another mile closer to the place and time that she would have to tell Philip good-bye.

When the train pulled into the station at Pusan, Philip slipped his arm about her waist and guided her down the steps from the train. He kept his hold on her while they made their way through the terminal and across the open plaza toward the taxi stand.

"Oh, wait just a minute. I can't let *Sahmonim* and Miss Jennifer see me looking like such a mess." She paused and brushed at her trousers, dismayed to find a rip at the knee, which must have happened when she fell. "I'm beginning to look more and more like a refugee."

"You look beautiful to me. Why do you care what they think, anyway? We're all pretty scruffy by now." Philip waved his free hand high in the air, keeping a firm grasp around Eun-Me's waist with his other. "There's Mom and Jennifer. Mom seems to want us to hurry. I wonder what's going on."

Sahmonim was waving frantically in the air, so they began to jog toward her. "We've got to rush to get to the pier. I'll explain on the way. We don't have time to wait for a taxi. We'll have to take a tram."

With Miss Jennifer in tow, *Sahmonim* led the way to the corner stop to wait for the next streetcar headed for the pier. Judging from the heavy smell of fish that filled the air,

Eun-Me didn't think they would have too far to ride. While they waited, *Sahmonim* began to explain the reason for the rush.

"We got off the train here in Pusan and were milling around the taxi stand with all the other missionaries, trying to decide what to do, when a young American soldier with the local KMAG approached us. He said that arrangements had been made for two boats to evacuate American citizens this afternoon and this evening. The others ran to catch the first one. If they left on time, they should already be at sea. But if we hurry, we can probably still make it aboard the boat that's scheduled to leave at six."

"That's not all the soldier had to say." Miss Jennifer interrupted *Sahmonim* as the trolley car approached their stop. "When he heard that I was going on to San Francisco rather than staying in Japan, he advised us to check the schedules as soon as we landed in Beppu."

She paused long enough to follow *Sahmonim* aboard the tram and grab hold of one of the safety straps that hung from overhead. "He said we ought to leave for America immediately if that was our final destination. They expect General MacArthur's army to be called in to settle this skirmish, and the seas will be teaming with troop carriers. According to him, any commercial ships that can, will want to leave the area as soon as possible. We may be on a freighter headed home as early as tomorrow. Wouldn't that be good?"

Even though Philip had guided Eun-Me safely aboard the tram, Philip's hand still rested on her waist, and she caught Miss Jennifer staring at his arm. The hint of a snarl curled her lips, and the flash of anger in the American's green eyes made Eun-Me squirm and want to pull away, but Philip gave her a gentle squeeze and drew her closer to his side.

"I'm not looking forward to leaving Mom and Grace so soon. And I'm not in any hurry to make that long voyage. I'm beginning to think that this journey will never end. However, the sooner you are safely home, the better. That's for sure."

Sahmonim's voice took on the tone she used when speaking to a child. "Now, Son, watch your tongue. We're all tired, but that's no excuse to be rude." Eun-Me couldn't keep the hint of a smile from playing on her lips.

The last trolley stop deposited them within several hundred yards of the pier. Several dozen Americans, both civilian and military, milled about the dock, making it easy for Eun-Me to immediately locate their outgoing vessel.

Along the gangplank leading onto the military transport that would ferry them across the East China Sea to Japan, a line had formed, and a stern-faced Korean port authority official checked passports and documents before permitting the passengers to board.

Everyone passed unceremoniously until Eun-Me stood before the clerk. He took one look at her and snarled in brusque Korean something to the effect that only Americans were allowed on board. A U.S. military policeman stepped forward from his guard post with his rifle poised. "Step aside." He barked the order into her face.

nine

Philip's hand on her back prevented her from instinctively following the command. "She's with me, and she carries the proper documents to allow her entrance into Japan. Show them your papers, Grace."

She turned her back on the men and fished the envelope from its secure hiding place. The official snatched the credentials from her hand and held them close to his eyes, then up toward the sun.

The clerk didn't bother to speak. He shoved the papers at her and jerked his head toward the boat. The American soldier stepped back and allowed her to join *Sahmonim* and Miss Jennifer, who were waiting for her at the top of the gangplank. Philip followed close behind.

"That's one fortunate little lady you've got traveling with you." A heavyset man in a business suit nudged Philip and ticked his head at Eun-Me while they stood at the railing with *Sahmonim* and Miss Jennifer. "We'll probably pass hundreds of Koreans at sea trying to sneak into Japan illegally. Those that make it that far will be caught and sent back." The stranger shoved his right hand toward Philip.

"Name's Conway. Joseph Conway. Own an import/export business back in the States. Was standing behind you folks in line back there. You're the only American I know who brought their *ajumoni* along for the ride to Japan.

149

You must have some pretty good connections to pull the strings necessary for such a thing. You aren't with the embassy, are you? No offense, but you don't look like a diplomat."

Eun-Me watched Philip as he tried to answer, but the man never paused long enough for Philip to respond with more than a shake of his head. An ivory toothpick bobbed from the corner of the man's mouth while he spoke, and he paused between sentences to suck air through his teeth.

"I hope you don't fancy taking her back to America with you. The permits she's got won't work. I'm always haggling with immigration officials, trying to get permits for my Korean business associates to enter Japan and the States. Entrance into Japan is difficult, but nigh on impossible back home." He pinched the toothpick between the fingers of his left hand and slid it from his mouth.

"We are aware of the immigration restrictions. She'll be staying in Japan." Philip offered no further explanation, but that seemed to be enough to satisfy Mr. Conway. He bit on his toothpick again while he backed away. "Listen, nice talkin' to you folks. I'm gonna see what they've got cookin' in the galley on this tub. Good luck to you all."

"A pleasure doing business with you, Sir," Philip muttered under his breath.

"Oh, children, that reminds me." *Sahmonim* pulled a package wrapped in newsprint from the top of her knapsack. "I forgot in all our rush to get to the boat. I knew you two wouldn't have had time to eat, so I bought some *kimbap* and dried squid as well as a few apples from the street vendor outside the train station while we were waiting for you. We can have our own little dinner cruise right here on the deck. Let's stake out that cozy spot over there." She pointed to an out-of-the-way corner that was protected by the overhang of the engine room.

"Count me out." Eun-Me watched Miss Jennifer crinkle her nose in a now-familiar way. "I think I'll follow that Mr. Conway to the galley. Maybe they have American food on their menu."

An earsplitting blast from the ship's horn echoed across the harbor and signaled their departure. From what Eun-Me could tell, she was the lone Korean passenger on a boat that didn't appear to be even half full. After the press of the crowds they'd endured all day, the relative solitude brought a welcome reprieve.

Against the backdrop of an evening sun melting into the sea's horizon, Eun-Me spread the simple meal out before the three of them, then Philip offered to pray. While he thanked God for the food and His watch care and protection throughout this long and difficult day, Eun-Me felt the ship pull away from Pusan's shore, and the burn of tears stung her eyes.

Only God knew what the future held for her homeland and when, or if, she'd be able to return. She swallowed hard against the rising knot of emotion that clogged her throat, as she echoed Philip's "Amen." Lifting her head, she watched her beloved Korea slip from view.

After dinner, Philip rounded up some blankets from a deckhand, and they made pallets under the stars. They'd no sooner gotten settled than *Sahmonim* announced she was going in search of Jennifer. She disappeared around the corner before either of them could volunteer to go for her.

"Grace, come with me." Philip stood and extended a hand to help her to her feet. Her body ached all over from her day's travails, and her spirit ached from emotional exhaustion, too. Yet, she didn't even consider refusing Philip's request. They had such precious little time left.

Together they walked to the railing, and Philip moved in close to her as they both looked into the ocean waves. "This may be my only chance to be alone with you before I leave. I suspect Mom was thinking the same thing when she hurried off. She wanted to give me a chance to tell you good-bye." Eun-Me's heart pounded wildly, and she had to breathe deeply to fight off the dizziness that the silhouette of his solemn smile produced.

"By most standards, this past week has been pretty awful. I certainly wouldn't have guessed when I left San Francisco just under three weeks ago that I'd be headed back to the States within a matter of days, racing to get my former fiancée out of Korea before the Communists cut us off." Philip gripped the railing tightly in both hands.

"I have to say, though, as strange as this sounds, that the lessons I've learned through this whole gruesome ordeal have made the trauma worthwhile for me. For one thing, I've gotten my priorities straight again. I'm committed to keeping my promise to return after my residency and serve as a missionary doctor, wherever and however God sees fit. I won't let anyone or anything deter me from my commitment to fulfill His call to follow Him."

He dropped his hands from the railing and turned to face Eun-Me, taking her hands in his. "Grace, there's another important lesson I've learned in the short time I've been here. . ." He paused and drew a deep breath as though the weight of his words clogged his throat. A shiver of anticipation ran through her as she waited for him to continue.

"I've been reminded of how valuable you are to me. I wouldn't trade this time I've spent with you for anything in the world."

He drew his face closer to hers, and she stared into his gray eyes. "I wish more than anything I could take you with us, but you and I both know that's not possible right now. I do vow to keep in close contact and will pray for you night and day. I promise. I'll be back as soon as I can." In a tender act reminiscent of his gesture earlier that day, he lowered his head and tipped her chin toward him. She closed her eyes and her lips prickled in anticipation of the kiss she was about to receive.

He gently kissed her, not once, but three times, each one lasting longer than the one before. When he pulled back from her, she longed to reach up and pull him toward her again, but she somehow found the discipline to refrain.

He watched her with such intensity, she knew he was waiting for her to respond. Yet, she groped for the right words to say. She had anticipated Philip's arrival for so long, but never in her wildest dreams or worst nightmares could she have possibly imagined that things would turn out like this.

She wanted to admit her love for him and confess that she had loved him for years. She longed to pledge to wait until he came back for her. She knew she couldn't or wouldn't marry another, even if Philip never returned. She would wait a lifetime for him.

Still, he hadn't come right out and said the words, "I love you." And, even if he did love her now, at least three years would pass until he would return. A lot could change before then. She had already exposed too much of her soul to him. The time had come for her to pull back and shelter her heart.

She averted her gaze and stared into the sea. "I think you know I share the same feelings that you've expressed. I wish we didn't have to say good-bye so soon, but knowing that you'll return gives me something to look forward to." She fell quiet, her thoughts, hopes, and wishes such a tangled mess that she couldn't sort through them.

They stood for a long time, feeling the brush of the salt-air breezes and listening to the ocean waves' rhythmic hammering against the boat's hull. The tempo reminded Eun-Me of an old folk song her mother used to sing to her, and she began to sing. Philip accompanied her by humming along, and his low tones combined with the sounds of the sea to soothe Eun-Me's frantic thoughts and frazzled nerves. Their voices tapered to silence when they reached the end of the tune.

❧

Wednesday, June 28, 1950

The boat's air horn jolted Eun-Me from her sleep as the first pink slivers of morning light danced on the ocean swells. She stood and looked across the water to see dozens of fishing boats heading out to sea. Tracing the wake of their boats, she saw the coastline of Beppu, Japan.

Japan. To Eun-Me, the very name represented bitterness. Resentment. Suffering. Fear. While the boat docked and they prepared to disembark, she prayed, begging God to bring a swift end to the conflict with the Communists so that she could hurry home.

The pier teemed with activity, despite the early hour. The sound of fishmongers screaming in Japanese as they hawked their catch made Eun-Me cringe. She hadn't stopped to consider that she'd have to revert to the use of Japanese. She'd tried to purge her vocabulary of the despised language after Korea was liberated from Japan's rule. Even though they had all been forced to speak Japanese in public and had been required to take Japanese names, she remembered with pride how her parents stubbornly continued to speak Korean in the privacy of their home. Eun-Me considered resorting to one of Philip's old childhood ploys to speak very fast in English when anyone addressed her in Japanese, pretending like she didn't understand one word of what they were trying to say.

Philip settled the women in an oceanside cafe and left them to eat breakfast while he went to check on the schedules of freighters heading for San Francisco. Eun-Me had no appetite. The realization of what this day might bring had just begun to sink in. Philip might be leaving her today. Leaving her alone with. . .alone with *Sahmonim* amidst a people she despised.

Philip returned and tossed an envelope onto the table in front of Miss Jennifer. "Just as you ordered. Two tickets for the *Maiden Voyage,* headed for San Fran." He pointed toward a rusty freighter anchored offshore. "You'll have to suffer with my company for just two weeks more—starting today. We're to be here at four this afternoon to board."

Eun-Me had to bite her bottom lip to hold back an escaping gasp. She could feel her life spinning quickly out of control. In less than a day, just hours away, Philip would be gone.

Philip gulped down a quick, now-cold bowl of fish soup and rice and pushed back from the table. "Mom, let's hope we can find this friend of dad's and get you two settled at his place before we take off. If not, we'll bring you back here to the evacuation center that our military has set up for all the Americans. They should be able to get word to Dad of your whereabouts right away, and I imagine we'd find the other missionaries there, unless they've decided to go on to Tokyo to wait."

"We'd better get going if we hope to be ready to leave by four o'clock." Miss Jennifer dropped her spoon in her empty rice bowl and stood. "Don't forget you promised to take me shopping before we left for America. I can't abide this dress another day!"

They walked out of the café and waited on the curb while Philip hailed two pedicabs. While he showed the first driver Tanaka *Hwangjangnim*'s business card to make certain that he could find the address, Miss Jennifer rushed to climb into the second cab beside *Sahmonim,* leaving Philip to share the cab with Eun-Me.

After a wild ride through a maze of pedestrian-clogged streets in the city's business district, their pedicabs turned down a narrow lane, lined on either side with walled courtyards, which surrounded traditional Japanese homes. They came to an abrupt stop in front of an unadorned iron gate, and *Sahmonim* caught up to Philip before he could set both legs out of their cab.

"Son, let me ring the bell and announce ourselves." She motioned him to sit back in his seat. "If he is home, Tanaka *Hwangjangnim* will recognize me."

From the open-air carriage, Eun-Me could hear the gate's chime echo through the small courtyard. Within moments, the sound of shuffling feet preceded the click of a latch. The gate opened just enough for the person on the other side to identify the caller, then it flew wide open.

"*Sahmonim! Ohsoh-oseyo!* Come in! Come in! What brings you to Beppu?"

Eun-Me's mouth fell open in surprise to hear the words of this white-haired, grandfatherly Japanese man, dressed in an American-style business suit, white dress shirt, and tie. He spoke in Korean and English, and not a word in Japanese.

"*Moksanim?* Is he not with you?" While *Sahmonim* explained that her husband remained in Korea but had sent his greetings, Tanaka *Hwangjangnim* craned his neck past the gate to peer into the two rickshaws.

"Please. Everyone, come in." He motioned to them, and Philip helped Eun-Me down.

"You must be *Moksanim*'s son. Philip, is it not? Your father spoke to me of you so often, I feel as though I know you well." Their host offered his hand in greeting to Philip and turned to give a traditional bow to Eun-Me and Jennifer. His English showed the stilted speech patterns and heavy accent of one who had learned the language later in life. "We must get you out of the street. Follow me."

He led them through the garden and slid open the lattice-work door, then waited for them to leave their shoes on the high step before ushering them into an austere room. Scattered cushions and a low table of black lacquer with an intricate floral design made of inlaid mother-of-pearl were the room's only furnishings.

"You must excuse," he said, gathering up an open Bible, notebook, and pen from the table. "My housekeeper does not work Wednesdays, so my home is a mess, and I have little to offer in way of refreshment." He pointed to the wall. "My dear wife, God rest her soul—you see her in the photographs there—she would have been embarrassed for visitors to find her house so."

Framed, grainy prints of a *hanbok*-clad, sweet-faced *halmoni* adorned the walls. In each picture, the woman's arms either held two babies or they were wrapped around a huddle of children. Eun-Me was beginning to feel as though she'd never left home.

Instead of taking a seat on the floor as Tanaka *Hwang-jangnim* pushed them all to do, she bowed deeply and said, "Sir, I am the Woods family's *ajumoni,* and I feel more comfortable working in the kitchen than having someone wait on me. If you would allow me the honor, I'd be happy to prepare some tea."

His nervous chatter ceased and relief showed in his smile. "You shouldn't have any trouble finding whatever you need. Everything is in full view," he said as he directed her to the tiny, alcove kitchen off of the front room. She lit a burner on the two-burner butane stove and set a kettle of water to boil. Then, making as little noise as possible, she gathered teacups from the open cabinet. On the countertop, a small ripe melon rested on top of a package of *dok,* and she took the liberty of arranging the rice cakes and fruit on a plate.

While she worked, she listened to *Sahmonim* explain to the gentleman the reason that her husband did not accompany them. Immediately upon hearing about their predicament, he insisted on them staying with him as long as they had need. He said that the guest quarters out back sat unused, and he would be grateful for the company.

"The place is far too quiet since my wife died." He looked longingly toward the photographs on the wall as he spoke.

He had read a day-old local newspaper report of the invasion yesterday, but the account didn't indicate any crisis of this size, and he had assumed that the fighting was just another border skirmish along the DMZ. Throughout *Sahmonim*'s account of the invasion and their hurried evacuation, Eun-Me heard him interject time and again, with an emotion-cracked voice, "My orphans. Oh, *Hahnahnim,* have mercy on them."

Guilt stabbed at Eun-Me's conscience as this elderly Japanese man expressed his love and concern for the Korean children he had devoted his life to serve. She had been so quick to judge and hate all the citizens of Japan for the actions of a few. She'd never stopped to consider that God can change the heart of anyone who comes to Him— even if he or she is Japanese—while evil wasn't limited to one race, but is found in every unrepentant heart.

Whenever *Moksanim* faced an obstacle in his ministry, Eun-Me always heard him quote the Scripture, *"All things work together for good to them that love God."* Could it be that God wanted to miraculously use this most horrid circumstance of war and her exile to Japan to perform a healing work in her soul? She sensed that, for her own spiritual good, He wanted and needed to purge her of the prejudice and hatred she felt toward the Japanese. And she feared she wouldn't have listened to His tug on her heart to repent had she not been forced into just such a circumstance as this.

Before she left the kitchen with the tea tray in her arms, she breathed a prayer of willingness, asking God to do His work of love in her heart and make her more like Him.

❧

Miss Jennifer showed no interest in refreshments and her frequent sighs betrayed her boredom at the never-ending talk of war. She threw repeated glances at her watch. When *Sahmonim* stood and asked the way to the facilities, Miss Jennifer seized her opportunity.

"Dr. Woods, we really should be going soon if I'm to have any hope of finding what I need before we disembark. As it stands now, I think we'll need to plan on going directly to the pier. I don't think we'll have time to come all the way back here."

Eun-Me threw a furtive glance at Philip, and her heart pounded in her chest to think that his departure was at hand. His mouth curved downward in a frown. "You won't give up, will you, Jennifer?" Although he addressed the American, he was watching Eun-Me.

"Son, her request is logical." *Sahmonim* laid a hand on Philip's shoulder as she spoke. "She does need at least a few basic necessities. And you did promise."

Philip shrugged his resignation. "Tanaka *Hwangjangnim*, perhaps you could direct us to a market where we can buy Miss Anderson some clothes. Her bag was stolen at the train depot yesterday, and she isn't prepared for an ocean voyage."

"If you don't mind, I'd be happy to go along and help you barter for the best price. If you go alone, they'll think you are tourists and raise the price considerably. Being Japanese, I am more likely to get a better bargain. Also, I'll be along to escort the women safely back here after they see you off."

"It's settled then." *Sahmonim* patted Philip's shoulder and moved toward the door. "We'll all go. Just let me freshen up a bit. I won't be more than a minute or two."

The teacups rattled in Eun-Me's hands as she cleared the refreshments away. "Here, let me carry that for you, Grace," Philip said as he lifted the tray and followed her toward the kitchen. They excused themselves from their captive host while Miss Jennifer regaled him with the tales of her agonizing journey.

"Perhaps you and I can sit in a café and talk while Mom and Tanaka help Jennifer shop." He set the dirty dishes in the sink, and Eun-Me began to pour the remaining hot water from the teakettle over them.

"I've been thinking, Philip. Maybe I should say my good-byes here instead of going shopping and to the pier. I don't imagine Tanaka *Hwangjangnim* would mind my staying behind in his home."

Eun-Me swished her hands through the sink water to avoid looking at him. She had made up her mind to try and handle things this way when he first handed the boat tickets to Miss Jennifer. Up until then, she had wanted to relish every last second she could have with him, but now she questioned the wisdom of abandoning all her customary reserve and allowing her emotions free rein. Each rich moment she had shared with him only served to increase her present pain. She knew she'd have to speak fast before she broke down.

"I can't bear the thought of making a public spectacle of myself like I'm afraid I would."

Already she could feel a huge knot forming in her throat, and he had to lean his good ear toward her to catch her whispered words. "A–a–and your leaving won't seem so final if I don't have to actually see you board the ship."

"Okay, Grace. I think I understand."

When she trusted her emotions enough to turn and look at him, she found her own pain reflected in his eyes.

Sahmonim's voice filtered from the other room. "Philip. Grace. Come on. We're all waiting."

"I'll be along in just a minute," Philip called out. "Why don't you three go on down to the corner to hail a pedicab?"

"Don't dawdle, Son. We really haven't much time." The sound of the others donning their shoes filtered through the open window.

"Oh, shouldn't I tell Miss Jennifer good-bye?" Eun-Me hurriedly dried her hands on a dish towel and started toward the door.

"I'll give your regards to her later, Grace. Let them go." He stayed her with his hand and lifted his head to listen for the house to grow quiet. Their voices trailed into the garden, followed by the clank of the gate latch. Philip bent to face Eun-Me and took her hands in his.

"I know you want to avoid a long, drawn-out good-bye, and I won't prolong the agony." Eun-Me watched the knot in his throat move up and down while he spoke. She could not look in his eyes. "I'll let what I said last night serve as my farewell."

When he leaned down so close to her that she was forced to meet his gaze, she startled to see tears shining in his eyes. She squeezed her own eyes shut tight and pursed her lips to try and stifle a threatening sob.

"Good-bye, Grace. God watch over you 'til we meet again."

His lips brushed against both her cheeks in gentle kisses, and when she opened her eyes again, he had gone.

❧

Eun-Me covered her face with her hands and tried to cry quietly at first, but she couldn't contain her pain. Rolling waves of grief swept from her in loud wails, and she dropped to her knees on the floor. Three years would pass at a slow, excruciating pace. And anything might happen in the meantime. Just this week she'd seen her life turned upside down in a few seconds' time.

The many crises of the past few days had not seemed overwhelming, as long as Philip had been there to share them with her. But now. Without him. She didn't know if she could bear her burdens another minute—much less three years.

At last, she reached the point of such exhaustion that she had no strength left to cry. Her weeping had weakened to hiccups when she rose from the floor.

Eun-Me reminded herself of one of the most important

lessons her *omma* had taught her. She could hear her voice saying the words, "When life's troubles are too hard to handle, one should keep thoughts and hands busy with work." So, she washed her face and tried to complete a few simple housekeeping chores. Yet, no matter how hard she tried to think of other things, her mind kept returning to Philip and the void he had left in her heart.

In anticipation of the Tanaka *Hwangjangnim*'s and *Sahmonim*'s return, she was in the middle of meal preparations when she heard the gate latch click. She quickly patted her eyes in a futile attempt to wipe away the traces of her crying spell and went to greet the visitor at the door.

Before her hand reached the handle, the door slid aside. There, alone on the stoop, stood Philip, a handful of brilliant pink *mugunghwa* in his hand. The sight of Korea's national flower surprised her almost as much as the sight of the bearer of the bouquet. She couldn't imagine where he might have gotten them, nor could she fathom what mission brought him back within two hours of saying good-bye.

Shucking his shoes at the door, Philip stepped inside and handed her the flowers. Eun-Me was speechless as he swept her into his arms. Her feet left the floor as he pulled her into a tight hug. Just then, she didn't care what brought him back, only that she was with him again. He loosened his hold so that her feet could once again touch the floor and backed away just far enough to look at her while he spoke.

"Grace, there's been a change of plans. I've been discussing them with my mom and Tanaka *Hwangjangnim*, but they all depend on you and we haven't much time, so I need you to hear me out before you respond."

Eun-Me couldn't have said anything at that moment, anyway. She still hadn't recovered from the shock of seeing Philip at the door. She nodded her assent.

"I love you, Grace. And I believe you love me, too—beyond just being best of friends."

Silent tears forced their way from her eyes, and she swallowed hard, confirming his supposition with another nod. He paused just long enough to smile, then took her bouquet of *mugunghwa,* set them on the floor, and took her hands in his.

"I can't bear the thought of being separated from you for a single minute. We've been through too much together to face the uncertainty of these coming days apart." He lifted a hand to her face and began to gently stroke her cheek.

"I've made some of the toughest decisions of my life this week, and I have you to thank for giving me the courage to see them through. You encouraged me to be honest with myself and examine my hopes and dreams and visions for the future. Because of that, I found the strength to sever a relationship that I now know would have only led to catastrophe for me. I'd lost track of what really matters and had allowed the lure of this world to blind me temporarily, but coming home and spending time with you reminded me of the important things in life—things money and status can't buy. I think God knew I needed you to keep me pointed in the right direction."

Eun-Me didn't feel worthy to take any of the credit he tried to give to her. She felt certain he would have reached the same conclusions eventually, as he allowed the Lord to speak to him and work in his heart. She started to shake her head and protest, but he laid a finger on her lips and silenced her before she could speak.

"I know you well enough to know that you feel self-conscious and insecure about your position as an *ajumoni* and lack of schooling and all. But, Grace, the spiritual wisdom you possess is far more priceless than a formal education, and your insight far surpasses mine. We complement and complete one another, you and me. I need you and I love you with all my heart. That's why I've come to ask you if you would be my wife." Philip fumbled in his shirt pocket for a moment, but never took his eyes off her. When he withdrew his hand from his pocket, he held his grandmother Carson's pearl-and-diamond ring.

"Grace, will you marry me?"

Eun-Me stared first at Philip and then the ring and then back to him. As much as her heart rejoiced to hear him proclaim his love for her, she feared that fatigue had made him lose all common sense. Finally, she found her voice.

"I love you, Philip. And I'd be so honored to be your wife . . .but I don't have anything to offer you. I'm orphaned and poor with no dowry to bring to a marriage, unlike Miss Jennifer. Besides, even if I said yes, I can't go to America and you must leave right away."

She dropped her head to hide the fresh sorrows that threatened to overtake her. She knew when he had time to think all this through, he would come to his senses and see the impracticality of his proposal. And when he did, Eun-Me would force herself to be content with the cherished knowledge that he loved her just as she loved him.

Philip tipped her chin up and gave her no choice but to look at him. "I won't take no for an answer that easily, Grace. Finish hearing me out. I haven't yet told you about my plan. While immigration laws won't permit a single, young Korean woman like you entrance into the States, they will admit you as my wife. And, even if we need a few weeks to get your visa approved, I've still got until September before I have to return." His words came faster and faster, and Eun-Me began to catch a glimmer of his hope as her own.

"Mom and I had a little discussion while Jennifer did her shopping. She offered to escort Jennifer to the States in my place if you agreed to marry me. And Tanaka *Hwangjangnim* offered to let us stay in his guest quarters as long as necessary. He'll take us to the provincial office to register our marriage right away so we can start your visa processing."

His eyes pleaded for understanding as he studied her face. "I don't want you worrying that you don't have a dowry and that your parents aren't living to arrange a marriage for you. When I told Mom I wanted to marry you, she said that she and Dad had often talked about who they would have selected for my wife had our family followed the Korean custom of matchmaking. And, Grace, they would have chosen you. Your name was divinely inspired, for grace is with you and you leave a remnant of that grace wherever you go. We all can see that the dowry you bring to our marriage is much larger than superficial, material things. Your inner beauty, spiritual strength, and giving, helpful spirit are worth far more than gold."

He dropped to one knee and took her left hand in his. "I'll ask you one more time before I say good-bye again and race to the pier. *Cho, Eun-Me, saranghaeyo.* Will you marry me?"

Eun-Me leaned to whisper in his good ear, "*Nye*, Philip. If you'll have me, I will marry you. Together, we'll pray that God brings us home to Korea soon, where we'll work side by side."

He slipped the ring on her finger and stood to pull her to him. She raised onto her tiptoes, circled his neck with her arms, and they sealed their covenant with a kiss.

Glossary of Korean Words

Ajumoni	(literally means "aunt") housekeeper
Anyong haseyo	(literally translated, "Are you living in peace?") Welcome! Greetings!
Ariyang	title of a traditional Korean folk song
Bulgogi	seasoned, grilled beef (a favorite Korean dish of many foreigners)
Dok	a sweet rice cake
Dong	neighborhood
Eye-go!	exclamation, i.e., "Oh, my!"
Hahnahnim	Almighty God
Hanbok	traditional Korean dress
Hangook saram	a Korean person
Halmoni	(honorific form: *Halmonim*) Grandmother
Haraboji	(honorific form: *Harabohnim*) Grandfather
Hwangjangnim	honorific title for orphanage director
Kamsahaomnieda	Thank you
Kebun	mood, state of mind
Kimbap	(sushi) seafood or meat rolled in rice and held together by a sheet of seaweed
Moksanim	honorific title for Pastor/Reverend
Mom-pei	everyday work pants
Mugunghwa	also known as Rose of Sharon; Korea's national flower
Nye	yes
Oh-pah	older brother
Ohsoh-oseyo!	Come in!
Omma	Mother
Opsumnida	"I have none," or "All gone."

Paksanim	honorific title for Physician
Pusan gachee sae-jang chusaeyo.	Four tickets to Pusan, please.
Sahmonim	honorific title for minister's wife
Saranghaeyo	I love you.
Sen-sei	Japanese title for Teacher
Shik-tang	restaurant
Yoboseyo!	Hello, is anyone there?
Yoh	sleeping mat

A Letter To Our Readers

Dear Reader:

In order that we might better contribute to your reading enjoyment, we would appreciate your taking a few minutes to respond to the following questions. We welcome your comments and read each form and letter we receive. When completed, please return to the following:

Rebecca Germany, Fiction Editor
Heartsong Presents
PO Box 719
Uhrichsville, Ohio 44683

1. Did you enjoy reading *Remnant of Grace* by Susan K. Downs?

  ❏ Very much! I would like to see more books
   by this author!

  ❏ Moderately. I would have enjoyed it more if

_____

_____

2. Are you a member of **Heartsong Presents**? Yes ❏ No ❏
 If no, where did you purchase this book?_____

_____

3. How would you rate, on a scale from 1 (poor) to 5 (superior), the cover design?_____

4. On a scale from 1 (poor) to 10 (superior), please rate the following elements.

_____ Heroine   _____ Plot

_____ Hero   _____ Inspirational theme

_____ Setting   _____ Secondary characters

5. These characters were special because _____

   _____

   _____

6. How has this book inspired your life? _____

   _____

   _____

7. What settings would you like to see covered in future
   Heartsong Presents books? _____

   _____

   _____

8. What are some inspirational themes you would like to see
   treated in future books? _____

   _____

   _____

9. Would you be interested in reading other **Heartsong
   Presents** titles?   Yes ❑   No ❑

10. Please check your age range:
    ❑ Under 18   ❑ 18-24   ❑ 25-34
    ❑ 35-45   ❑ 46-55   ❑ Over 55

Name _____

Occupation _____

Address _____

City _____ State _____ Zip _____

Email _____

Heirloom Brides

*L*ove and faith are the greatest of inheritances.

These four closely related stories will warm your heart with family love and traditions. Each bride has a legacy of faith to leave with generations to come. And the heirloom chest will forever be symbolic of their love.

paperback, 352 pages, 5 ³⁄₁₆" x 8"

❤ ❤ ❤ ❤ ❤ ❤ ❤ ❤ ❤ ❤ ❤ ❤ ❤ ❤ ❤ ❤

❤ ❤ ❤ ❤ ❤ ❤ ❤ ❤ ❤ ❤ ❤ ❤ ❤ ❤ ❤ ❤

·······Presents·······

Great Inspirational Romance at a Great Price!

Heartsong Presents books are inspirational romances in contemporary and historical settings, designed to give you an enjoyable, spirit-lifting reading experience. You can choose wonderfully written titles from some of today's best authors like Peggy Darty, Sally Laity, Tracie Peterson, Colleen L. Reece, Lauraine Snelling, and many others.

When ordering quantities less than twelve, above titles are $2.95 each.
Not all titles may be available at time of order.